WAGON CAPTAIN

E. E. HALLERAN

SAGEBRUSH
Large Print Westerns

First published in Great Britain by Hammond
First published in the United States by Ballentine

First Isis Edition
published 2020
by arrangement with
Golden West Literary Agency

A catalogue record for this book is available
from the British Library.

ISBN 978–1–78541–699–6 (pb)

Published by
F. A. Thorpe (Publishing)
Anstey, Leicestershire

Set by Words & Graphics Ltd.
Anstey, Leicestershire
Printed and bound in Great Britain by
T. J. International Ltd., Padstow, Cornwall

This book is printed on acid-free paper

CHAPTER
ONE

The May sunshine was warm on the wet earth; it brought up little wisps of steam from the muddy pools and churned ruts of the Overland Trail. Three days of spring rains had bogged the great stream of westward traffic, slowing the ceaseless flood that pushed on toward the Rockies. The wagons were on the trail early this season, everyone seeming to realize that this would be a year of mass emigration. Appomattox was thirteen months in the past and the nation was ready to resume its push to the west. Mud on the trail was just something to be endured.

A tall man on a rangy mouse-colored mule splashed his way forward along a line of floundering freight wagons, pausing briefly to exchange comments with each driver in turn. He was almost as muddy as the laboring mule teams but he did not seem to mind any more than the animals did. Early season travelers along the Oregon and California trails had to take a beating from the elements but it was part of the game, to be foreseen and accepted with no more than the usual grousing. Ross Sheldon had estimated the troubles of the expedition, weighing them against the expected advantages, and was prepared to accept what came.

He reined in to keep pace with the lead wagon, grinning quizzically at the moon-faced driver, who handled his six wallowing mules with heavy-handed deftness. "Keep a weather eye behind you, Baldy," Sheldon cautioned, "in case any of the boys get bogged down. I'm going to shove on ahead and take a squint at the lower crossing." The grin faded from beneath the close-cropped mustache as he spoke.

Baldy Cope nodded, his round little eyes narrowing in the broad face until they were mere slits. "I'll watch 'em, Ross," he promised. "But why go to the trouble? We figgered fer Julesburg all along. The Californy crossin' will be a mess after all this rain. Even Moses couldn't ha' prodded the Israelites across there without losin' half the tribe."

A brief smile flickered across Sheldon's lean countenance; it was Baldy Cope's habit to find a scriptural reference for every occasion. "I'm still planning on Julesburg," he assured his partner and lead driver. "A float job's the best bet but it's smart business to have a look at every possibility."

Cope nodded again and ejected a spurt of tobacco juice across the muddy flanks of the nearest mule. "Better save some o' that steam, Ross," he cautioned soberly. "Purty soon ye'll git over bein' mad at her and ye'll have yerself all wore out."

Another of those fleeting smiles came and went. "I forgot her a week ago," Sheldon declared.

Cope spat again. " 'Ye're a dad-ratted liar, Ross. Ye've been drivin' yerself ever since we left the Missoury. Ease up a bit, man!"

2

He had to shout the final admonition. Sheldon was already urging his rawboned mount forward along the line of slippery ruts, grim eyes studying the rolling horizon ahead. Even on a mule the man wore an air of brisk efficiency. He rode like a cavalryman but with a looseness that hinted at habitual readiness.

He swung away from the muddy trail to avoid the worst of the morass left by churning wheels and struggling hoofs, and soon came within sight of the Platte's broad yellow surface. He had to come to grips with the problem of crossing. Many train captains chose the California, or lower crossing, partly because it was shallow and partly because they wanted to get the ordeal behind them. Sheldon had other ideas but he didn't propose to miss any opportunities.

He edged a little closer to the stream, marking how the rains had caused it to inundate the lowlands along its normal banks. Never a deep river, its dangers were a muddy bottom, quicksand and shifting holes. In its present state of flood there would be the further difficulty of added width. The first man who had claimed it to be a mile wide must have seen it at this stage of flood.

He climbed one of the low swells which fringed the river, seeing the densely packed mass of wagons a mile or so ahead of him. Travelers were jamming up on the near shore, some of them waiting for a slackening of the waters while others double-teamed for safer but slower passage.

There was just time for him to note the half-dozen struggling teams in the river itself and then his attention was caught by three skulking forms much nearer at hand. In one of the gullies which led toward the river a man held three ponies while two other men crept along toward the stream. Sheldon recognized the two crawling toward the river as Indians, probably Pawnees, while the horse-holder was either a breed or a white renegade. There were many such gangs along the trail now. Army deserters, former guerrillas and other outscourings of the war had moved west to throw in with those Indians who retained the old urge to war on the white invader. The Indian menace was pretty much a thing of the past in this part of Nebraska but criminals of both races still contrived to prey upon emigrant trains.

Sheldon reached under the skirts of his loose brown coat and pulled his gun even as he urged the mule forward into the swale. He could not see what the two skulkers were trying to do but he recognized them as the natural enemies of both freighter and emigrant. Anything he could do to break up their game would be a move in the right direction.

He checked the loads of the long-barreled Colt's English Model, making certain that caps were snug and the balls rammed in properly. By that time he was able to get a brief glimpse of the trio's intended victim. Someone was coming along the river bank just beyond the little ridge which flanked the broad stream. Evidently the dismounted Indians proposed to catch the stranger by surprise at the point where gully and river met.

4

Sheldon sent the mule at a dead run through another draw but the ground was too flat for full concealment. The horse-holder spotted him as he rounded a low hill, a quick yell of warning and a carbine shot sounding in quick succession. Sheldon heard the whine of the slug as he turned to ride straight at the horse-holder, blasting a shot from his revolver as he drove in.

Without waiting to see the size of the attacking force both Indians turned and ran back. The third man flung himself into a saddle and galloped to meet them with the led horses. In two minutes all three of them were digging heels into their ponies and disappearing behind the ridge.

Sheldon was satisfied. He slowed his mule to a walk and angled out to meet the unknown rider. He even smiled a little at memory of the renegades' panic. Highwaymen along this part of the trail were not made of very stout stuff. Mostly sneak thieves. A good scare usually kept them at bay. Still this pair had been pretty bold in venturing an open attack.

Then he broke out along the river bank and knew the reason for their boldness. The intended victim had been a woman. She was less than a hundred feet away when he got his first good look at her and he was instantly puzzled. This was not the sort of woman to be found wandering along the Platte. She was, he guessed, in her middle twenties, dressed almost like the pictures he had seen of society women on fox hunts, and mounted on a fine thoroughbred roan. She had hesitated briefly at sight of him but now she came on, her expression one of aloof annoyance. He decided that she had a pretty high opinion of herself — and not without some reason. Her oval features were perfect and her chestnut hair showed a hint of curl beneath the broad-brimmed hat that was her only departure from Eastern garb. It seemed a shame that her severe expression had to spoil the picture.

"What is the meaning of this?" she demanded as she pulled up where he had blocked her path. "Were you shooting at me?" Evidently she had not seen the Indians.

He shook his head. "Couple of Pawnees and a breed had an ambush for you. I happened to spot 'em and they dusted out." When she looked skeptical he added, "You'd better get back to your outfit, ma'am. This isn't healthy country for stragglers, especially women."

She stared at him coldly, disdain in her brown eyes. "Am I to believe that you became sort of a . . . straggler yourself just so you could drive away three desperate thugs and offer me a kindly warning?"

He looked at her steadily. "I don't care much what you believe. I'll just repeat the warning that you'd better get back to whatever circus you strayed away from. I wouldn't bother to repeat for any man — even a greenhorn — who hinted that I was a liar."

"You're impertinent!"

The tight little smile flickered across his lips. "That makes us quite a pair," he said, bowing slightly. "Me impertinent, and you a spoiled brat. Now turn that fancy horse and skedaddle back to your outfit before I take a strap to you like your pappy should have done years ago!"

He kneed the mule toward her and for an instant he saw fear mingle with anger in the dark eyes. Then she whirled her horse, sending mud flying in all directions as she headed back upstream. It pleased Sheldon to ride after her since he was going in that direction anyway.

She looked back once and he could see her give the bronc a couple of sharp cuts with her riding crop. He had a hunch that she didn't like the idea of having a despised longear keep pace with her thoroughbred — so he spurred the mule along just to show that it could be done. Hitting at her pride seemed like a fair way to get even for her show of scorn.

He let her go when she swung away from the flat, riding on at a normal pace to come within sight of the tangled mass of wagons at the Platte crossing. At least forty canvas-topped vehicles were crowded on the top of the bluff while three others were being lowered to the river bank. He could count ten at various stages of the actual crossing, all of them double-teamed but still having troubles.

He sat his mule in silence for a good ten minutes while he studied the work of the freighters in the river. Far out toward the far shore he could see where a pair of wagons had fouled each other in deep water before being upset on a sand bar. Close to midstream another outfit was evidently in quicksand, and others were having more routine troubles. But still the wagons went into the stream, as others coming down from the bluff almost forced them to take the plunge. Julesburg would certainly be better than this.

He had already noted the big W painted on the sides of the wagons ahead so he rode in to inspect them at closer range. This would be the new Winthrop outfit he had heard about back at Leavenworth. He wanted to see how a big company handled such a problem as the crossing of the South Platte.

This was a well-equipped train. The wagons were new and the mule teams were made up of sturdy animals. On the bluff and as far as the river bank the organization seemed good. Only in the river were they having troubles — and that could happen to anyone.

A man hailed him as he came in among the waiting teams. "Hi thar, Ross. Lose yore outfit?"

He waved a casual salute, recognizing the muleskinner as a fellow named McLarnin. "They're back along the trail a piece, Mac. Looks like the Platte's real rambunctious today."

McLarnin drew on his corncob pipe before replying, "Never seen it wuss. Too shaller to wade and too deep to swim — or mebbe I got it backwards. Glad I ain't boss right now; it's a bellyache!"

Sheldon grinned and rode on toward the spot where heaving teamsters were trying to get a wagon started into the silt. A massive redhead was bossing the job and doing the work of three men at the same time. Sheldon halted, watching the redhead until the wagon slid away. Then he saw the two horsemen who had been watching from the other side of the vehicle. One of them was a man of about his own age and size, a lean, wiry sort of fellow who was muddy enough to look like dozens of others along the trail. At his side, however, was a stout

8

man who looked completely out of place. His clothing was much too good for the occasion and he had evidently kept carefully away from flying mud. Sheldon guessed that the heavy man was in his middle fifties, a pompous-looking individual who would have appeared more at home in an office than in the mud of the California crossing.

The redhead turned then and saw Sheldon. "Ye bringin' yer outfit up, Ross?" he asked.

Sheldon shook his head. "I'll not crowd you, Fawcett. We're headed for Julesburg."

"Be swift there," the redhead warned.

"We're figuring, on it. Rather have that than what you're stuck with here."

The stout horseman broke in abruptly. "What's this about Julesburg? I thought the upper crossing was too deep for wagons like ours."

"Lots of folks figure that way," Sheldon told him. "Every man to his own choice. So long. I've got to get back to the train."

He rode up the bluff, letting the mule rest for a minute when they reached the higher ground. It gave him a chance to hear a faint *plink-plink* somewhere back along the line of waiting wagons and he was grinning broadly as he rode toward the sound. Presently he saw the man who was making it, a short, squat fellow who had apparently decided to make use of the delay by tuning up his banjo. When he was directly beside the man, Sheldon murmured sorrowfully, "It's no use, Smoke. If you ever get that thing tuned up it'll just make your singing sound that much worse."

The stocky man looked up with a grunt of surprise, his broad grin showing broken teeth. "Danged if it ain't Lieutenant Sheldon!" he exclaimed. "Big as life and twice as muddy. What's the idea. Lieutenant? You ain't gittin' to be no lawyer out here."

Sheldon imitated the other's nasal tenor. "I ain't gittin' to be no lieutenant neither. Baldy Cope and I went partners in a freight outfit. We're right behind this train, planning to make a float crossing at Julesburg."

"Wish I'd knowed about you and Baldy. I'd-a been after a job."

"I just saw McLarnin up ahead. He knew about us."

"I ain't seen Danny to talk to since we left the Missoury. In a crowd this big you don't git no time to be sociable at all." He plinked a banjo string as though to indicate what he meant.

Sheldon chuckled. "I see. Mac has been staying out of earshot. What about the other poor pilgrims? Can you get any of 'em to listen?"

Smoke grinned amiably. "I'm gittin' 'em broke in gradual. You know how it was that winter at the relay station. Folks kinda git used to it."

"Or go crazy. Where's this outfit headed?"

"Fort Laramie. Winthrop's fixin' to set up a store there. But you didn't tell me how come you quit lawin' and turned to freightin'."

"Plans changed," Sheldon said shortly. "The lady didn't seem as enthusiastic about me as she did when I went away to be a war hero. I guess she expected me to come back with medals and all I showed up with was a bad disposition and some saddle sores."

The wagons had been moving up as they talked, leaving a small gap in front of Smoke Prine's team. Suddenly a voice snapped from behind Sheldon's shoulder, "You'd better get on about your business, mister! You're holding up this wagon!"

Sheldon turned to face the lean man he had seen by the river. "Sorry," he said. "But don't get worried about it. Smoke will be up there long before they're ready for him."

"Don't tell me my business, mister! We don't like strangers snooping around our wagons."

Sheldon studied the hard gray eyes and decided that the man was not the greenhorn he looked. "You got a mortgage on this piece of trail?" he asked.

"I got enough to —"

Sheldon cut him short. "I'm going, Windy," he said in an even voice. "But don't think I'm going because you sounded off. I'll even give you a bit of advice before I go. The next time you feel like giving me orders — don't!"

He sat his mule quiet but tense, watching the way the other man's hand hovered around the butt of his six gun. There was a moment of flat, menacing silence but then the other rider turned his horse and rode back toward the river.

"Who was that?" Sheldon asked over his shoulder.

"Dale Enright. Kind of a clerk. Winthrop's puttin' him in charge of the Laramie store. Acted real tough, didn't he?"

"Maybe he is."

"He backed down."

"I wonder? . . . Well, sing him a song for me. It'll serve him right."

He eased his mule back along the line of wagons, noting that many of them carried freight but that some were hauling emigrant families and their property. Evidently Winthrop was really planning to set up an establishment at Laramie.

Almost at the end of the line he saw the girl in riding garb again. She had tied her horse at the back of an emigrant wagon and was inside with someone who appeared to be ill. The driver of the vehicle was a gaunt man with an unkempt beard and patched overalls, so Sheldon decided that the girl did not belong here. She looked out just in time to catch his eye, and he raised his hat courteously and rode on toward the fork of the trail. He did not expect a reply to his greeting and he did not get one. Which suited him well enough. He seemed to have the knack of antagonizing every woman he met. Maybe he ought to avoid them entirely.

CHAPTER
TWO

Sheldon's wagons made their noon halt almost opposite the approach to the California crossing and he was tempted to visit the Winthrop train for another look. His better judgment warned him against it so he rode back along the trail, discovering that an emigrant outfit was coming up pretty fast. Accordingly he spent the afternoon trying to hurry his own teams along. It was always good policy to have a fair gap between trains. Then a halt for repairs would not mean losing place in the line. For a freight outfit that was important.

By nightfall they were three miles farther upstream, the mud making any better progress impossible. As usual they forted up for the night in the style of the old fur trains. On signal the train would split into two columns, the odd numbers left and the even numbers right. When the two divisions were abreast of each other there would be a second halloo and the lead wagons of each file would turn in sharply, halting as their teams were about to pass each other. Numbers three and four would angle in a little less sharply, teams going to the inside until they were screened by the wagons ahead of them. A similar maneuver would be carried out all along the line until the numbers nineteen and twenty closed up the rear of the long rectangle. It put the entire train into a defense position without lost motion, every team except numbers two and twenty being inside. When these two were led into the enclosure the train was secure against both direct attack and stampede attempts. Here along the South Platte there was no great danger of such troubles but Sheldon had made it a point to use the formation every night since leaving the Missouri, drilling his teamsters against the time when it might be important to have the habit firmly established.

Camp was uneventful, men and animals weary enough so that sleep came as soon as the evening meal was over. In the morning the routine was picked up quickly and the train slogged onward, Sheldon inspecting every wagon both before and after it took its place in line. This phase of the journey was simply a matter of continuing the battle against mud and distance. The big thing was to keep going, to avoid unnecessary delays from breakdowns or other troubles.

They made somewhat better progress as the mud began to dry out a bit and at the noon halt Sheldon went scouting once more, this time for a look at the Julesburg crossing. To his satisfaction he found the river still high, so high that two emigrant trains had halted on high ground to wait for slacker water. The passage he had been keeping in mind was clear of wagons and within the hour he was signaling his own teams into position along the bank.

Sheldon issued only brief orders; most of the men knew what they were to do. Twenty wagonloads of potatoes would bring fancy prices in the mountain country at this season of the year but quick delivery was important. Prices would begin to fall as soon as the first supplies began to roll westward. This crossing was to be the spot for gaining time on other trains and each man knew what was expected of him and why it was important to do it properly.

They were unloading before the last wagons pulled into position, sacks of potatoes being laid out on boards provided for the purpose. The deep wagon boxes had been caulked before leaving Leavenworth and would float half a load without trouble. At Julesburg the South Platte was a river rather than an expanse of quicksand shallows and Sheldon had planned accordingly. Instead of sending loaded wagons to wallow across he proposed to float them over. Even making two such crossings for each wagon would be simpler and faster than the usual method.

Now a teamster named Eli Ludlam took charge. He was popularly reputed to have been a deserter from the Union Navy but Sheldon knew him only as a good wagon man who had worked for a time on a Missouri River steamboat. Back in Leavenworth they had discussed a plan for making the Julesburg crossing and how Ludlam was going to have a try at making good his boast that he could handle it.

He went to work with some skill even though he insisted on shouting a lot of nautical commands which he then had to translate into language the muleskinners could understand. They cursed his "belays" and "avasts" but carried on just the same. Every wagon carried the usual long rope, generally used for double teaming on steep grades but now to be used for a different purpose.

The plan was to have a double team secure a footing on the far shore with a line across the river to help drag several swimming teams at once. They knotted a number of their ropes together to form a line judged long enough to span the river even at the severe angle that was bound to result when the powerful current swept the first outfit downstream. The line was fastened to the back of the first wagon, which was then launched some distance upstream from their point of crossing, not only double-teamed but escorted by men on extra animals. They watched anxiously as the mules moved out slowly into deep water, and Sheldon began to feel uneasiness as he saw the force with which the current took hold of the desperately swimming animals in midstream. The line played out with frightening speed, but Ludlam's estimates held good and the first team struggled up into the shallows of the far shore not only with line to spare but almost directly across from the rest of the wagons.

So far, so good, Sheldon thought with relief. While the outfit across the river rested up, he got the first group of wagons ready for the haul across. They were able to make a chain of five wagons before their supply of ropes gave out, but this seemed enough for the first attempt, which would necessarily be a trial run. Sheldon signaled to the men on the other shore and the lead outfit started up onto dry land, towing the five swimming teams behind them.

There was an anxious interval when the current began to drag the first tows sideways against the pull from either shore and there was another bad moment when the last wagon was whipped downstream but finally the whole line began to move steadily, the teams on the far bank aiding the swimming ones.

"Shame we didn't fetch extry ropes," Baldy Cope lamented. "This here's the best trick since Moses forded the Red Sea."

Sheldon was already lining up wagons for a second trip. The South Platte had a nasty habit of rising and falling rapidly and without warning. He wanted to get as many wagons across as possible while the flood stage made the new scheme practical.

Ludlam's team came back with an empty wagon, bringing only their ropes, and once more the strategy was carried through. This time the men knew a little more about the job and they handled it briskly. Still it was getting pretty dark by the time the second group of five wagons made the crossing and Sheldon called it a day. The plan was working well but it was no game to try in the dark.

Luck held good and in the morning the float operation went on apace, this time with two-way crossings as unloaded wagons returned to pick up the half-loads they had left behind. It meant that they had to make forty loaded crossings and twenty returns to get twenty wagons over, but men who had made other Platte crossings did not complain. They were getting the entire job completed in less than a day's time, whereas many trains were delayed at the Platte for a week. At the same time they were avoiding the lost cargos and broken wagons which so often resulted from getting into quicksand.

Shortly after noon they were reorganizing on the north bank, the drivers reloading their wagons and thinking up cutting remarks to aim at Ludlam, who was feeling pretty cocky. The ex-sailor didn't let it bother him a bit; he had let them know that a salt-water man could handle a "piddlin' little crick."

"We'll haul out to the north-side trail," Sheldon told them. "That'll get us a place in line in case any outfits have come across at the lower ford. Then we'll re-grease all axles and make sure that the mules didn't take any harm."

"Water done 'em good," Ludlam yelled across the camp. "Even bilgewater could sweeten up a mule — not to mention some muleskinners I know of."

"Aye, aye, Admiral," Sheldon called back. "Anchors aweigh; we won't make Laramie on wind."

The train moved out in high spirits, the men enjoying the banter as well as the feeling of triumph at their passage of the South Platte. Sheldon rode along the line to look for signs of mechanical trouble but by the time they halted along the rutted pathway north of the river he felt reasonably secure.

He was even a little proud of himself. Smart planning had gained his outfit at least a full day on the Winthrop wagons. In a competitive business like freighting that was quite an item.

He sat back to watch the wagons going into corral, enjoying the snap and precision which the drivers were

18

displaying. It was only when the outfit was forted up for the night that he saw another man watching with equal interest. The fellow sat his horse at a little distance but the clothing marked him at once. It was the stout man Sheldon had seen at the wagon camp downstream, the man he had guessed to be Winthrop himself.

For several minutes Winthrop paid no attention to Sheldon, contenting himself with his study of the wagon movements. When the job was complete and the outside teams were taken into the enclosure he rode across to ask abruptly, "Is that your idea of how to camp a wagon train?"

"No." Sheldon was equally abrupt. "It's Jim Bridger's."

"Learn it from him?"

"Sure."

"In the army?"

"In what passed for an army out this way."

Suddenly the stout man chuckled. "Giving me a dose of my own medicine, are you? No offense intended; I just get a bit short when things go wrong — and they've been going plenty wrong with me. You're Ross Sheldon, aren't you?"

"I am. Why?"

"You talked to Red Fawcett a couple of days ago. A couple of the drivers in my outfit have talked about you. They said you'd get across the South Platte in a hurry. I rode up here to see."

Sheldon didn't mind bragging a little. "We came up from a couple of miles behind your train. Looks like we're ahead now."

"Mind telling me how you did it?" Winthrop seemed interested rather than annoyed at his successful rival.

Sheldon told him, explaining the differences between the Julesburg and the California crossings. The stout man followed the explanation carefully, nodding his understanding.

"Sounds like you did some smart planning ahead of time. Sorry I didn't find somebody like you to handle my train."

"Fawcett's a good man," Sheldon told him.

"I suppose it's not his fault. I picked the lower crossing and he tried to carry out orders. It was my mistake. Now we're in a mess. Half of our wagons haven't even started across. We've lost two beyond redemption and we stand to lose a couple more. Fawcett and Prine were both so sure that you'd make this Julesburg crossing that I had to ride on ahead to see if you turned out to be as smart as they claimed. After seeing the way your train operates I'm convinced. Now I've got a proposition to make."

Sheldon smiled, partly at the compliment and partly at the nervous way Winthrop talked.

"At the moment it looks as though we won't be clear of that infernal mud for another week," Winthrop went on. "Meanwhile I've got most of my equipment on this side, lying idle while we wait. I'll give you three hundred dollars to take the first half of my train on to Laramie while I stay here and try to salvage the remainder."

Sheldon frowned in surprise. "You're taking a chance on a stranger, mister," he said slowly. "All you know about me is that I made a river crossing in a hurry."

Winthrop shook his head. "I talked to Prine. Remember? I know that you were an officer in the Iowa Cavalry and that you were on patrol in this country all during the war. You know the trail better than most people and you know how to handle wagons. I can see that with my own eyes."

"You make my war record sound almost respectable," Sheldon replied, the quick smile showing for an instant. "Actually I commanded a lot of fellows like Prine. Good men but with no discipline, no uniforms and mostly no pay. More desertions than medals. Don't take my war experience seriously."

"I'm not trying to buy medals. I'm just tired of having my outfit run by men who don't know their business. The offer stands."

Sheldon considered it for a moment. The fee would be clear profit and very useful to the new freight company. Nor would it be a bad idea to establish good relations with Winthrop. If the stout man proposed to set up a trading post at Fort Laramie he might be a good prospect for future contracts.

"There's one big objection," Sheldon said finally. "I'm already in business for myself. I'm hauling potatoes, figuring to get high prices from folks who haven't had anything but salt pork most of the winter. The first loads to reach them will knock the top off the market. Naturally I don't propose to neglect my own train to help any rival ruin my market."

"That's sensible," Winthrop agreed. "I've got a few loads of potatoes in my train — or I did have. At least one load rolled over on a sand bar so there's one lot of competition you don't need to worry about." He let a wry smile show momentarily on his round face but went on hastily, "I'll undertake to send no potatoes with you. Will that get around your objection?"

"I'll ask my partner. He'll have to take full responsibility with our wagons if I leave."

"Let him know that it's not competition," Winthrop persisted. "I'm planning to set up a freight depot and trading post near Laramie. It'll be big and it'll be permanent. Almost a third of my train is hauling materials for construction and it is those wagons I want hustled forward. If we're to get the place set up this year I've got to get men at work."

"I'll talk to Baldy," Sheldon said. "Come on over."

He broached the subject to his partner without preliminaries. "There's the offer. It's up to you. If you think you can handle the train alone I'll take it. Naturally the fee is to be split like any other partnership earnings."

Cope squinted thoughtfully. "No bad river crossin's ahead. No reports of Injun troubles. Only thing is it don't leave us any spare driver."

"I'll send you one," Winthrop volunteered. "I've lost at least two wagons in the river and I already had a couple of extra men along."

"Deal then," Cope said. "It's kinda fun to be a Good Samaritan when ye kin make a profit doin' it."

"Very well," Sheldon agreed. "Three hundred dollars and no potatoes."

Winthrop smiled. "Deal. Come on back to my camp with me. We've got plenty to do."

22

Sheldon went to pick up his bedroll and then they were moving back toward the California crossing, having agreed to send the extra teamster in the morning. He would overtake the train before Cope would need to do any scouting.

Winthrop talked animatedly as they rode, evidently well pleased with the deal he had made. Sheldon was content to listen, partly because he wanted to learn all he could about the train he was to handle and partly because he didn't want the stout man to think he was too anxious for the job.

He learned that the Winthrop train had originally left Kansas City with fifty-two wagons, a dozen of them loaded with equipment and tools for the proposed construction work. Others carried the usual trade materials demanded by both Indians and settlers, about half of the total number being laden with canned goods. Many of the teamsters were really settlers who could not afford their own outfits. They were working passage for themselves and their families by driving teams and with promises of work on the buildings that were to go up.

Sheldon wondered about the girl he had seen across the river but he decided not to ask a direct question. There was a more important matter to be settled and he didn't want to leave any doubts about it.

"Who's in charge of these wagons now?" he asked. "You will have someone going along to take charge of your construction, of course, so we'd better have an understanding before we start. Divided authority is no good."

23

"Don't worry on that score. I'm sending my daughter as my personal representative although my chief clerk will probably handle most of the duties at Laramie."

"This clerk isn't a fellow named Enright, is he?"

"He is. Why do you ask?"

"Because I had a few words with him the other day. I doubt that we'll get to be real good friends."

"I'll guarantee that he won't bother you. I told him off pretty soundly after his meddling caused some of the trouble at the ford. He'll be under your orders at all times. I'll see that it is understood!"

"Is your daughter the only woman with the train?"

"With this part. The emigrant families are still on the other side of the river. She will also be merely a passenger."

Sheldon didn't argue. If Miss Winthrop turned out to be the girl he had met along the river bank there would be some question about her taking his orders but it didn't seem like a good idea to borrow trouble.

"Just so we understand each other," he said quietly.

CHAPTER
THREE

Sheldon had a chance to meet his new crew around the supper fires, discovering to his satisfaction that both McLarnin and Prine were among those who had made the crossing. Prine had been with him during most of the war and McLarnin had spent one whole winter on stage patrol with them. Both men knew the country and would serve to anchor a green crew.

He made the rounds of the fires, discovering that his old friends had been bragging him up rather extravagantly. He passed it off as a joke but was glad enough to have it so. It would make it easier for him to assume command.

Neither Miss Winthrop nor Enright joined the others around the fires and Sheldon judged from the remarks that no one missed them. He got only a fleeting glance at the girl but it was enough to tell him that he had guessed correctly. She was the same one he had exchanged words with before.

When supper was over he moved back to discuss details with Winthrop, noting that Smoke was getting out the banjo. The stout man pointed, chuckling. "Here goes our minstrel."

"I've heard him called worse," Sheldon said. "Mostly in good humor."

"That's the way it is here. Everybody complains about his singing but they all crowd around to listen."

"He was our private war horror," Sheldon said. "Got a voice like a handsaw hitting a nail and he can't keep his banjo in tune. The only song he knows is 'Oh, Susannah' and he never sings that one twice the same way, either in words or tune. It's pretty terrible but he manages to lighten up a journey. Makes for what sailors call a happy crew."

"That's it exactly. The men make fun of him but stick close to hear what his next job is going to sound like. I'm a little sorry he's going with you; I'm getting so I look forward to his performances."

Tonight Mr. Prine was being very modest with his humor, a variation from his usual bawdy style. Perhaps his habits were improving, Sheldon thought, having been influenced by traveling in a train that included several women. Smoke gave his instrument a few preliminary whacks and set his raucous tenor to the task of commemorating the problems of the California crossing.

The emmy-grants all wet their pants.
They're not ashamed o' that.
They're sweatin' blood to fight the mud
That fills the derned old Platte.
From Mis-ser-ee to Lar-a-mee
There's lots to make us sick,

But nothin' worse to make us curse
Than fordin' this damn crick.

There was a prompt and enthusiastic chorus, the volume of sound serving as a sort of applause for the verse.

Oh, Susannah! Don't you cry for me.
I'm headed west, a doggoned pest
With a banjo on my knee.

Sheldon laughed. "I see the Prine performance has become such a standard that the chorus has taken a part in the show. That's good. This crew will work well together with that kind of spirit."

The fun continued for perhaps a quarter of an hour, most of the verses being old Prine jobs that Sheldon had heard before. Then Winthrop called for attention and explained his reasons for sending Sheldon ahead with a part of the train. It was just a formality, since everyone already knew, but it served to put Sheldon in official charge.

The younger man took his cue, speaking seriously to the teamsters. "Three rules in my train," he said. "I want them observed by this one because they're good rules. We corral every night in fur-trader fashion. We examine axles and other gear before and after every stream crossing. We keep the train closed up. My job is to see that these rules are carried out. Your job is to keep the wagons rolling. Starting time is starting time for everybody. Everyone understand that?"

The nods were general and he went on, "Every wagon is to be loaded at daybreak tomorrow. Drivers make sure that your teams are ready for a fast haul. We've got time to make up. We'll pull out as soon as I've had a look at each outfit. Get your breakfasts tomorrow morning while I'm doing the looking. That's all."

He waited to see if anyone had a comment, then went back to where Winthrop was standing. "How many wagons will go along?" he asked Winthrop.

"I don't know. Take all you can."

Sheldon didn't press the point. It was beginning to be clear that one reason for Winthrop's troubles was that he didn't know how to handle his own affairs.

He traded a couple of friendly insults with Prine and then turned in for the night, picking a spot under a wagon where no one else had staked a claim. At the break of day he was up and about, noting that his orders were already being carried out. The loose gear around the camp was being loaded swiftly enough and many of the teams were ready to span in.

He made a hasty breakfast with Smoke Prine, turning at once to the job of inspecting wagons and assigning numbers as each outfit was declared fit for the trail. Each driver was cautioned to keep his number in mind as it would be used night and morning when the train corraled or moved into action. McLarnin drew the number-one spot while Prine was held for the rear-wagon job, his number not certain until it could be determined how many outfits would make up the train.

Winthrop watched from a distance, talking to his daughter and to Enright while Sheldon went about his business. The wagon which appeared to be the Winthrop headquarters was saved until last and Sheldon checked it without speaking to the waiting trio. When he found everything in order he nodded to the lanky graybeard who seemed to be the driver. "You're number eighteen. Follow Burkett. He's got seventeen. You know about night camps, don't you?"

The old man winked broadly. "I got it. When Burkett pulls out to the left I haul to the right and close up behind sixteen. Don't ye worry none about old Jesse."

"Right." Sheldon turned to Winthrop and reported, "Looks like nineteen ready to go. Two need repairs and three more carry spuds. I'm ready to roll."

"What about extra mules and a stock man?" Winthrop asked.

"I'll take a half-dozen mules but we'll lead them singly behind wagons. No point in taking an extra man. You might need him here."

"Suit yourself. Before you go I'd like you to meet my daughter Harriet. She understands the nature of our agreement." He added after a moment of hesitation, "I believe you've already met Enright."

Sheldon offered her a polite but rather stiff bow. He guessed from her tight expression that she half-expected him to mention that they had met before — and he suspected that she did not want her father to know. "If you're riding a wagon you'd better climb aboard," he said, speaking to neither one specifically. "We're moving."

He turned away, signaling for McLarnin to hit the trail. The response was prompt and he had the satisfaction of seeing other wagons wheel into line with almost no confusion. There were plenty of good drivers in this company; all they needed was a little organization.

When number eighteen moved into line he saw that Miss Winthrop was on the seat beside Jesse, waving a brief farewell to her father. Enright had mounted a big roan and was riding forward along the far side of the train.

"Nice work," Winthrop said at his elbow. "Looks like I was right when I decided to gamble on your ability. That's the smartest show I've seen from my wagons thus far."

"Thanks. Good drivers like it that way. I think we'll make Laramie in good time."

He turned to mount his mule but Winthrop halted him with a gesture. "One thing more, Sheldon. Do you have any commitments to any of the traders in this country?"

"Nothing very big. Why?"

"I'm thinking about the future. Maybe you can guess why I decided to come out here and set up a trading post."

"The usual thing, I suppose. The country is going to build up."

"It's bigger than that, my boy. Maybe you don't think I'm much of a man. I'm sure the way I've let my train get behind is nothing I can brag about. But I suppose I'm looking to the future more than to the present. I know for a fact that the much-discussed railroad is going to be built. It will go through this country, almost certainly through Laramie. That's why I'm making my move. In another year or two the long freight hauls will be a thing of the past; wagons can't compete with railroads. I'm planning to be in a position to take a profit from that situation."

Sheldon frowned. "So soon?" he asked.

"I'm sure of it. You fellows on the long trail will be out of business."

When Sheldon did not reply he went on quickly, "I've closed out most of my business along the Missouri because I believe the freighting business is going to become a matter of handling the short hauls from remote settlements to railroad centers. That's why I propose to get myself established at one of those centers. You could be just the fellow I need to handle that local hauling trade for me. You're a good wagon man and you know that country. Think it over between now and the next time I see you. Maybe we can work out some kind of a deal that will be of advantage to both of us."

"Sounds like an idea. I'll keep it in mind." Sheldon climbed to the back of the sleepy-looking mule and picked up the reins. "One other thing. I see Enright's riding loose. Does he undertake any duties with the train?"

"He's been doing a bit of scouting. I don't know that he'll be any good to you but he seems to fancy himself in that capacity. Don't worry about him."

It wasn't a very definite answer but it seemed to be the only one that would be forthcoming so Sheldon let it go at that. He waved a casual salute and sent the mule in pursuit of the rolling wagons.

The morning's haul was uneventful and he had a good opportunity to think about what Winthrop had told him. If the railroad came through so quickly it meant an upheaval in his plans. The whole idea annoyed him, not because he felt that he could change the progress of the country but because he seemed to be heading for another of those interruptions which had marked his life during the past few years. The war had broken in on his law studies. His assignment had thwarted his sudden ambition for military glory. The girl who had promised to marry him had changed her mind while he was out riding escort for mail coaches. Partly because he resented so much of the past he had gambled on going into the freight business — and now that was threatening to blow up in his face.

He tried to be reasonable about it, telling himself that his annoyance was largely emotional and that his prospects were really pretty good. Winthrop seemed to know what he was doing and Winthrop's plans seemed to include Ross Sheldon. Things might work out pretty well.

They made their noonday halt just short of the spot where the Sheldon-Cope wagons had camped after the Julesburg crossing. It had been a good morning's journey and Sheldon was well pleased. He went among the drivers while they were boiling their coffee, making certain that each man knew his instructions for forming the corral. He made it plain that no trouble was to be anticipated along this part of the trail but that the practice might be important later. No one disputed him and he decided that Prine and McLarnin had really built him up to the other drivers.

Enright did not come in for the noon breather and Sheldon pretended not to notice. When he dropped back to talk with Smoke in mid-afternoon, however, he asked, "What's this Enright up to, Smoke?"

"Danged if I know," Prine confessed. "He's a real queer one. One day he'll be pizen mean and the next he fair sickens you with his soft talk. I reckon he's after somethin' but I dunno what it is."

"The Winthrop girl, maybe?"

"Don't seem so. Mostly they don't git together at all."

Late in the afternoon Sheldon let the train go past him while he took a look at the gear. This time Smoke had a companion. Enright had come in from his scouting activity and was riding along beside Prine's wagon, apparently on good terms with the squatty man. It puzzled Sheldon but he did not comment. Smoke could handle his end of the matter.

At dusk they made a very decent corral, only two wagons having to back up and correct errors of spacing. For a first attempt it was a remarkably good job and Sheldon took pains to tell them so. He had been lucky to get started on the right foot and he proposed to keep it that way as long as possible.

Another morning saw the train moving out smoothly and Sheldon rode ahead to study the trail as soon as he saw that the camp was properly cleared. Enright galloped up to overtake him. Sheldon nodded and kept going, the two of them riding side by side in silence until Sheldon pulled the mule down to a walk. Enright promptly did the same with his roan.

"Sorry I shot off my face the other day, Sheldon," he said without preliminary. "I thought you were just a prowler."

"No harm done."

"I just wanted to tell you. No use having any hard feelings. I'm just a clerk with this outfit but I'm willing to do anything I can to help. Just say the word if you want me to do anything at all."

"Thanks. After we cut across to the North Platte there'll be some chance of being annoyed by renegade Indians. We can use your scouting services."

"Glad to do it. I'm no plainsman but I'll try to follow directions."

"You can get right at it now, if you like. That'll let me stick with the wagons a bit more."

"Right. What do I do?"

"Just ride out about a half-mile ahead of the wagons. Look for anything that we ought to know about before we get to it. I'll relieve you in a couple of hours."

Enright nodded and put spurs to the roan. Sheldon pulled aside and let the mule rest while the wagons came up. He was puzzled by Enright's sudden show of friendliness, wondering what had caused it.

He traded comments with each driver as the wagons rolled past him, noting that the brisk spirits of the previous day still showed. After the troubles at the lower crossing the men were glad to be moving.

When number eighteen came along Miss Winthrop was on the seat as before, dressed much as she had been when Sheldon had seen her for the first time. She greeted him formally. "Will there be any objection from the train captain if I ride my horse?" she asked.

"No objection if you remain with the train," he assured her. "Would you like me to bring your horse around?"

She jumped from the wagon without replying or waiting for Jesse to halt. Sheldon watched while she slipped the knot of the big bay thoroughbred that had been tied at the back of the wagon, already saddled. Almost as quickly she was in the saddle, swinging wide of the trail. That suited him well enough. He didn't mind her arrogance as long as she didn't demand special treatment.

He waited until she had ridden forward along the column, greeting various drivers as she passed them, and then he swung in beside Smoke, riding close so they could converse without shouting.

"Looks like ye're on speakin' terms with the lady," Prine commented. "I figgered ye'd git around to it. She's a real purty gal."

Sheldon grimaced. "She's got a disposition like a Cheyenne medicine man. I'm more interested in Enright. What did he talk about yesterday when he was back here with you?"

"Mostly about what it was like out this way durin' the war. Why?"

"This morning he turned up all peace and good will. I wondered what brought about the change."

"He was kinda that way with me," Prine said slowly. "Seems like Winthrop told him how ye'd been ridin' these trails all durin' the war and he wanted to know if ye'd ever got up into the Powder River country. He seemed real interested when I told him we'd both been at Fort Connor."

"Get any idea what he really wanted?"

"Nope. Couple o' times I thought he was goin' to ask about some people special but both times he kinda backed water. Playin' it smart, I reckon."

"We'd better do the same," Sheldon told him. "I think he's trying to pump one or both of us. We'll play innocent and wait for him to do the work."

"Right with me," Prine agreed. "And don't be so grouchy with the Winthrop gal. Remember she's one gal in a gang o' men. It ain't likely she's goin' to let herself git too free and easy."

It was a point Sheldon had not considered. It surprised him that Smoke had thought of it. "I'll be good," he promised with a grin. "It's easier that way."

CHAPTER
FOUR

The train continued to make good time with the weather remaining fine and trail conditions excellent. Enright seemed determined to prove himself as a scout and on several occasions he consulted Sheldon about sign he was unable to read. He listened to Sheldon with keen interest, asking questions about Indians and Indian habits until it seemed clear that he meant to get well acquainted with the subject. Not once, though, did he show interest in the Powder River country.

Miss Winthrop was equally diligent. She made it a point to patrol the column when it was in motion and twice she spotted minor troubles which might have caused delays if they had not been detected promptly. Sheldon began to feel that he had judged both of them wrongly.

Three days took them across the dreary expanse which separated the two branches of the Platte, the ease of travel compensating for the heat and the monotony. Each evening Smoke entertained with his "music" and spirits continued high. Once a westbound stage passed them and twice they met eastbound coaches but otherwise they had the trail to themselves. All reports from the stage drivers indicated a quiet season. The government's new Indian policy was apparently bringing peace to the troubled regions north of Laramie.

On the fourth night they camped along the North Platte, half a day's march above Court House Rock, and Smoke put on a particularly raucous concert, closing with a new — and very modest — tribute to himself. As usual, its tune bore a faint resemblance to "Oh Susannah."

When wagons roll along the trail,
They need a leader fine,
And a danged good man to ride the tail
And keep the rest in line.
Most any greenhorn on a hoss
Kin scout fer Injun sign,
But it takes a damn good man to boss
The tail like Smokey Prine.

The usual chorus was blotted out by howls of disparagement but Smoke kept banging away at the banjo until they chimed in with the usual,

Oh Susannah! Don't you cry for me.
I'm headed west, a doggoned pest
With a banjo on my knee.

The general good humor seemed to affect Miss Winthrop. She came across to where Sheldon lounged against a wagon wheel, asking abruptly but with a smile, "How many days to Laramie, Captain?"

He looked down at her with an answering smile. "If we're lucky — five. Better call it six. Why?"

"I'm trying to make some plans. Time is important with a project like ours. The big problem will be to get construction started. I must set up the sawmills and get the timber cutting started. I'll also have to protect the stores while the buildings are going up. It all takes a lot of planning."

"Sounds like you've worked on this kind of operation before," Sheldon told her. "You're figuring details that some folks would forget."

"I lay claim to reasonable intelligence," she retorted. "Please omit the compliments and tell me about the timber situation around Laramie. Is it so far away we'll have to put up temporary sheds until the regular work can be done?"

He let the fleeting grin cross his lips. "Sorry I sounded human. The timber around Laramie is no good. You'll have to count on a week or so before you'll have time to get in any building timbers from the hills. But don't bother to build sheds. Dismount the wagon boxes from the wagons that are to be used in hauling the logs. It'll be easier and quicker to use the boxes for your temporary storage."

"Thank you. That's exactly what I wanted to know." She turned and left without ceremony.

Somewhere behind him Sheldon heard a man mutter, "Don't that gal beat all! Fer a purty one she's shore a bundle o' ice."

Sheldon spoke over his shoulder without looking at the other man. "Don't criticize the lady. She's got a nice even disposition — always nasty."

Next morning Sheldom went out ahead, trying to pick the best trail for the wagons. Much of the ground was so rutted that it was often better to leave the regular trail and seek easier travel. Because of the number of rock ledges and gullies there was a risk involved so he was being extra cautious about it, paying little attention to the train itself until he happened to see a pair of riders moving away from the rear of the column and angling off toward the famous Chimney Rock formation which loomed on the left. He realized that the riders were Miss Winthrop and Enright but he thought little of it, knowing that travelers frequently rode across for a closer look at the odd spire of rock. It was only when they disappeared completely that he understood what they were about. They were going to ride completely around the rock.

He was tempted to give chase but it would be bad judgment to leave the train unguarded and there would be no chance of catching them when they had so much of a start. He compromised by riding across to the high ledge which fronted the rock, thus putting himself in a good position to watch the wagons and at the same time move toward a spot where he would be able to look around the formation from the far side. Since the wagon trail made a long arc around the spire he could stay ahead of the train and still be in a position to lend assistance if the wandering pair ran into trouble.

Apprehension was making him rather touchy by the time they appeared in view. Their path had actually been a little shorter than that of the train and they were coming out a little ahead, in spite of the detours they had made around the rocky ledges. Miss Winthrop was flushed with the excitement of the mild adventure and evidently quite pleased with herself but Sheldon ignored the smile she gave him, staring grimly at Enright.

"From now on," he snapped, "you will kindly omit foolhardy trips like this one! There is no excuse for putting Miss Winthrop in danger."

The other man bristled. "Don't take that tone with me, mister!" he exploded. "Your duty is with those wagons. Stay with them and mind your own business!"

"Please!" Miss Winthrop protested. "We don't want any bickering."

"And we don't want any casualties," Sheldon told her. "You had one warning about the dangers of straggling. Don't make me speak of it again."

"So far as I am concerned," she said clearly, dark eyes flashing, "it will not be necessary for you to speak to me again — on any subject."

She sent her pony into a run as she angled toward the wagon train. Enright delayed only long enough to shoot a malicious grin at Sheldon. Then he followed.

That night Smoke came up with a new verse. He hadn't talked to Sheldon about the incident of the morning, partly because Sheldon had kept entirely to himself during the day. The regular duties had been carried out as usual but there was an unaccustomed silence all along the line. Wagon men knew that Sheldon had taken the wanderers to task and they could sense the air of hostility that had resulted. As a result the camp had been rather subdued, Smoke's first verses getting little response. Then he used the new one.

> There's lots o' pilgrims on the trail.
> They go from here to there.
> They're hardy sons who carry guns
> To try and save their hair.
> It don't seem right to fort at night
> But risk yer scalp by day.
> There's Injun knives to take the lives
> O' them what stray away.

The chorus didn't even get started. Miss Winthrop was striding wrathfully across toward the singer even before the final line came out.

"Did Mr. Sheldon put you up to that?" she demanded.

Smoke didn't get a chance to reply. Sheldon's voice boomed across the fires, "Better ask that of me, Miss Winthrop. Not that it makes a bit of difference. It's good advice. You can take it or let it lie."

Out of the corner of his eye he saw that Enright had risen as though to take a hand in the argument but Miss Winthrop settled the issue by turning sharply and going back to her wagon. Enright promptly sat down again.

There was an uneasy silence for the space of a couple of minutes. Then Smoke plinked the banjo a couple of times, winked at Sheldon, and launched into one of the old nonsense verses. It broke the tension a little but no one relaxed very much. The good humor of the train had suffered.

For two days the train rolled on in dour silence, a long day of rain not helping morale at all. Scott's Bluff and Fortification Rocks fell behind. Sheldon exchanged no word with either Miss Winthrop or Enright during that interval. Twice they picked up bits of news from passing stagecoaches but the news was evidently good. The Laramie Council, called by the Indian Bureau, was already being organized and the report was that even the more reluctant Sioux were coming in to make peace.

On the night of the twenty-sixth of May they went into formation on the north bank of Cold Creek, having used their last hour of daylight to ford the stream. They had just settled down to a good supper after the usual camp chores when a rider came splashing across the ford from the south. He proved to be a dispatch rider carrying messages to the peace commissioners at Laramie. Of more interest to Sheldon was the fact that the courier was an old acquaintance, a grizzled civilian scout named Hanna. The man had been rated as an excellent scout but in his army service he had been just as distinguished for his tendency to gossip. Hanna could be counted on to report everything from market conditions to the temper of the hostile tribes.

Sheldon shouted a brisk invitation to supper and the lanky old scout waved an acceptance, attending to his horse before coming over to shake hands all around.

"Figgered to ketch ye somewhar along here, Ross," he said. "Got a couple o' things to ax ye. Hiyah, Smoke. Still bein' a earache with that damned banjo?"

Prine showed his broken teeth in a delighted grin. "How's the army's oldest errand boy?" he inquired. "Too bad they give up usin' drummer boys out here; you might make it if'n ye could learn to keep yer nose clean."

Hanna took the tin of stew they handed him, wolfing it between acid remarks aimed at Smoke Prine. Sheldon was curious to know why Hanna had greeted him as he had but he knew that the man would get to the matter in his own good time. Temporarily he was relieving the camp's tension with his humorous attack on Prine.

One of the teamsters was not so patient. He broke in to ask, "What's what with this peace talk? Ye said ye was goin' to the commissioners?"

"That's what I said, all right. And that's where I'm headed. Got a message fer 'em. A fool message, I'd call it." He looked about him as though to make certain that his audience was listening, then added, "This fool gov'ment gits crazier every day. The Injun Department is demandin' that the army keep shady and let 'em talk the redskins into bein' nice boys. They don't want no troops around this part o' the country 'ceptin' enough to ack like Injun police. But the army has got a regiment on the way out here to git tough. Somebuddy back east ought to make up their minds!"

"I heard that the Powder River region was to be occupied," Sheldon told him. "Is that what the new troops are supposed to do?"

"Ye kin figger it thataway, and the commissioners at Laramie are plumb riled. They sent word to Colonel Carrington that they want him to keep his sojers away from the post. Troops might make the friendly little red rascals uneasy. I'm takin' Carrington's answer back to 'em. He'll keep clear. Plumb disgustin', ain't it?"

"Suits me well enough," Sheldon told him. "My outfit's hauling supplies to Laramie. It's easier to sell when there's peace."

"Where at is Baldy Cope? I hearn tell he was partners with ye."

"He's up ahead with our wagons. These wagons belong to the Winthrop people. They had trouble at the California crossing and I'm handling part of the train so as to save time."

Hanna nodded solemnly. "I hear tell about that too, now that ye mention it. Bad luck fer them was bad luck for yerself. It put ye within earshot o' Smoke — and that ain't fittin' to happen to no man."

They all laughed and Hanna paused a moment to enjoy the success of his remark. Then he spoke again, more seriously. "What do ye know 'bout Major Twiss er Milo Crabiel er John Richards, Ross?"

"No more than anyone else, I suppose," Sheldon replied in some surprise. "They're all renegades of a sort."

"I don't mean that. Where was they at when ye heard about 'em last?"

"Let me think a minute . . . I don't believe I heard anything of Twiss after he deserted to the Sioux at the time of the Connor expedition. He just disappeared completely. Crabiel was in pretty much the same class, though we did hear some talk at Fort Connor that he'd been seen up in the Big Horns a couple of times. Richards was still doing business near Sage Creek in September, peddling whiskey to the Indians and getting away with it. You can put old Joe Bissonette in the same class if you want to add a name to your list. What's up?"

"I dunno fer sure. Seems like the gov'ment's got a hunch that some Rebels stirred up the Injuns durin' the past few years. They got a real purty young feller comin' out to look into it and he axed me to pick up anything I could. Seemed like ye might know somethin', bein' as how ye was with Connor."

"I wasn't with him long and I didn't hear any talk like that."

"Got any opinions?"

"I'll make a guess — for what it's worth. I'd say that Richards and Bissonette are just outlaws who'll do anything for money. Twiss and Crabiel sound like better suspects. What they did doesn't make sense any other way, but Richards and Bissonette were whiskey and gun peddlers long before the war."

"What about French Pete?"

"He's honest — and he's a smart trader. He gets along with the Indians because he has a Sioux wife but he knows he can't make a decent profit unless there's peace."

"Right. I'll pass the word to the purty boy when I git back."

Enright broke in with a question. "Is there any real reason to think that the Confederacy paid agents to arouse the Indians — or is that just some more political imagination?"

Hanna turned to stare at him from beneath shaggy brows. "I ain't the one to say, mister. I'm jest passin' along the talk."

"Maybe Mr. Enright can help, Sam," Sheldon said dryly. "He seems to have quite an interest in the subject."

Enright came up from his seat as though on a spring. "Who says I do?" he exploded.

"We're not exactly blind," Sheldon reminded him. "You've been listening to Sam here with your eyes bugged out. You have quite an interest in the Powder River country —"

"That's a lie! I never . . ."

Sheldon took a couple of quick steps to face him at close range. "Easy with that kind of talk, Enright!" he warned. "I don't like being called a liar."

"Then lump it! I say you lie!"

Sheldon took another step and Enright went for his gun, eyes blazing as he jammed its muzzle against Sheldon's belly. "Stop right where you are!" he ordered. "I'll not take any bullyragging from you or anybody else!"

A flat silence fell across the camp as Sheldon stared curiously down at the weapon which menaced him. For a couple of seconds the only sound was the crackle of the fire but then Sheldon remarked in a casual voice, "You're getting a little wild, aren't you, Enright? What's the matter? Don't you want people to know you're on Crabiel's trail?"

He could see the other man's start of dismay so he followed his advantage, staring into the darkness and snapping, "Don't shoot, Smoke! He'll come to his senses."

Enright bit. As he whirled to defend himself against the imaginary threat, Sheldon sprang. Sweeping the gun down with his left hand he smashed a hard right to Enright's head. The man went down and rolled over, groaning. Sheldon picked up the gun and tossed it to Prine. "Give it to him when we get to Laramie," he said calmly.

Everyone settled back then, trying to pretend that nothing had happened. Enright slouched away to his blankets and Sheldon steered the talk back to the bitterness of the Sioux against the Bozeman Trail. It was a topic on which all could agree. The trail would be held by force of arms or not at all.

Smoke summed it up with a verse evidently concocted while the latter stages of the talk went on.

To deal with varmints like the Sioux
Don't make a bit of sense.
They'll strip ye bare and take yer hair
To hang up in their tents.
The only talk a redskin heeds
Is talk made with a gun,
So chase the blame commission-eers
And bring on Carring-ton.

Hanna grinned delightedly while the chorus did its duty. Then he rose and stretched. "Sometimes ye almost make sense, Smoke," he conceded. "Not that it makes yer noise sound no better."

"Give me credit," Prine said. "It ain't often you find a voice what jest matches an off-key banjo."

Hanna was gone when the train moved out next morning, a general air of expectancy pervading the whole company. Laramie was not far ahead but the talk of Indian trouble put everyone on the alert. With Indians converging on the post there was almost certain to be a risk of meeting a few wild bucks who would be on the prowl for trouble. Because of that Sheldon stayed out ahead of the train, first warning everyone to be alert at all times.

He saw Indian sign several times and twice spotted moving bands of Indians but the day passed without any trouble and they pulled in on the south side of Laramie River just as dusk closed down.

The night passed with only one brief alarm and in the morning Sheldon went to Miss Winthrop's wagon and spoke to her for the first time since their argument. "My contract ends when we cross the river. Have you made arrangements for the next move?"

"Not yet. I must go to the fort and find out where the ground is that my father arranged to occupy."

"Better do it right away. I might as well head the train in the right direction — if I can find out what direction that is."

"Thank you. I shall report to my father that you carried out your contract to the letter. My personal opinions have nothing to do with that judgment, of course."

"Very fair of you, I'm sure," he told her, bowing mock-formally.

CHAPTER
FIVE

The Laramie crossing was a simple one and Sheldon promptly turned the train over to McLarnin, telling him that Miss Winthrop would give orders about its final destination. By that time he could see the girl coming back from a hurried trip to the fort, so he waved her a casual salute and turned away. It was time he started taking care of his own business.

It didn't take him long to see that the point of land between the Laramie and the North Platte was filling up. Most of the flat between the ramshackle fort and the river was occupied by shacks and tents of all descriptions and across the stream the tepees of the visiting Indians were beginning to make quite a showing. The conference was not expected to start for at least a week but already eager tribesmen had gathered for a quick portion of the white man's bounty while equally eager traders were setting up their shops for the expected rush of business.

He circled the worst of the tangle, heading for the old established trading post of Bullock and Ward. Cope had spanned out his wagons behind the long storage sheds and wagon corral of the company, so Sheldon assumed that his partner had already made some kind of deal.

Baldy was waiting for him, a quizzical grin on his broad features. "Seems like ye hustled them greenhorns along mighty brisk, Ross. We crossed the local Jordan jest before dark last night. Ye almost cotched us."

"They're not all greenhorns. Smoke and McLarnin are with 'em, along with some other good men. The others picked up fast. Got a deal with Bullock?"

"Nope. I ain't the dickerin' type. I left it fer you. Bullock knows we're here, though."

"Fair enough. I'll go right in and see him." He swung down from the mule, turned the animal over to Cope and walked around to the front of the trading post.

The place was bustling with activity as Indians came to trade. Tobacco, rice, sugar, coffee, peppermint candy, bright calico, gay ribbons, knives, brass-headed nails and glass beads were bartered briskly for furs, leather goods and the various Indian trinkets which were beginning to find an eastern market. Bullock and Ward had gained a reputation for fair dealing among the Indians and the scene scarcely vindicated Hanna's gloomy predictions. There was an infernal din arising from the squalls of papooses, the haggling of white speculators, the alternate *Wash-tal-la* and *Wan-nee-chee* of the Indians as they showed either satisfaction or the opposite. Still it was an orderly sort of babel, the redskinned customers showing signs of good humor as they bargained with Bullock's clerks. Sheldon knew that Colonel Bullock always had clerks who could speak Cheyenne and Sioux as well as English. That always helped in dealing with Indians.

After a few minutes of observation he caught Bullock's eye and the lanky trader came across to greet him. "Yo' want me, suh?" he inquired politely, his Southern accent strong in spite of his years on the border.

"I've got eighteen wagons of potatoes," Sheldon said bluntly. "Want 'em?"

Bullock nodded. He was a tall, spare individual with a goatee that seemed determined to out-jut the angular nose. His easy, courteous manner sometimes led greenhorns to take him for, an easy mark but few of them made the same mistake twice. Seasoned frontiersmen as well as the Indians took him for what he was, an honest man whose word was as good as his bond.

"We can use almost anything we can get this yeah," he said. "How much did yo' figgah to ask for yo' load?"

Sheldon made a sudden decision. "Prices will depend on whether people arrive here faster than provisions do. How'd you like to take them on commission?"

Bullock eyed him curiously. "Mostly the freight lads want to sell for a quick profit. What did yo' have in mind, suh?"

"A couple of things. You're a dealer and I'm a freighter. You'll know how to make the best of the seller's market around here. The other idea is that I expect to stay in the freighting business. You're an old firm and I'd like to continue doing business with you."

"When could yo' delivah?"

"Right away. The wagons are already behind your sheds."

"Oh, those wagons. I thought the were twenty of 'em."

"Two are promised to French Pete. I made the promise last fall and I like to make good on my word."

"Eighteen will be fine. Can you unload or do I have it done?"

"We'll do it. The potatoes are sacked; it'll be easy."

"Good. Yo' want a deposit down?"

"Enough to pay my men. The rest can wait."

Bullock smiled. "Yo' seem to place a lot o' confidence in us, suh. Have Ah met yo'?"

"A couple of times. I'm Ross Sheldon, formerly lieutenant, Seventh Iowa. I was in and out of here pretty often during the past four years."

Suddenly Bullock seemed to understand something. "Then yo' pa'tnah is that scriptuh-quotin' rascal Baldy Cope! He was in last evenin' but he didn't allow as he had anything to sell. Didn't even tell me he was with the wagons Ah saw comin' in."

Sheldon chuckled. "Baldy's afraid his conscience wouldn't let him drive a hard-enough bargain. He lets me do the dirty work. Wait till he hears what I did!"

They laughed, shook hands, and moved back into a sort of office where Bullock counted out enough coins and bank notes to let Sheldon meet his mid-trip payroll. There was no writing between them. Sheldon liked that. No one stood to lose by dealing with Bullock and Ward, especially if the deal was understood to be a real gentlemen's agreement.

Baldy Cope didn't question the decisions even for a moment. He simply went to work at the task of rounding up men to move the wagons into the Bullock yard for unloading. It didn't take long. Men who wanted to get loose with pay in their pockets could make short work of such a chore.

Bullock came out once, to see if arrangements could be made to have the Sheldon-Cope train carry a couple of loads of furs back East. That was exactly what the partners wanted and the terms were settled promptly.

Sheldon took care of several other points while the men worked. He found two of them willing to forego a mid-journey fling to earn extra money as camp guards. Eli Ludlam had already agreed to take one of the wagons up to French Pete's post above Bridger's Ferry. Sheldon would handle the other wagon himself so everything seemed squared away. When the men were paid and the company broke up the partners found time to congratulate themselves on their first trip. They had made a good profit, picked up the extra fee Sheldon had earned from Winthrop, and were in contact with the best firm of traders in the West. For a new outfit just going into business they hadn't done badly.

"I think you'd better move out as soon as you can pick up loads," Sheldon told his partner. "Eli and I will need a good fortnight to make the delivery at French Pete's. There's no point in losing time. Pick up anything that will pay its way but don't haul anything else. If

55

we're going to make any money in this business we can't let folks get to thinking that the eastbound trip is deadhead. Get on the trail as soon as you can. You'll have no difficulty in picking up a second load along the Missouri. Two trips this season will set us up good."

"Ye think I oughta go without ye?"

"You brought the train out without me most of the way. This time you'll have veterans with you — if you don't lose the boys on either end. Give 'em a couple of days to bust loose but keep an eye on 'em so you can pick 'em up again. Most of 'em will be anxious to get back on a payroll."

Cope grinned. "Prodigals soon git tired o' their husks. Mebbe it's lucky fer freight outfits that the world's so full o' prodigals."

They settled the other details and Sheldon moved away to make his preparations for the trip north. He would have preferred to stay with the train but a promise was a promise. In this case it was also good business. If the Bozeman Trail could be opened to regular travel a spot like French Pete's would be a profitable one. Getting Pete's hauling business would be worth the effort.

Just before supper Smoke Prine ambled in, his banjo slung over one shoulder, his bedroll and slicker over the other. He grinned amiably at Sheldon and asked, "Ain't lookin' fer a good man what kin handle mules or music with equal skill, are you?"

"You quit the Winthrops?" Sheldon asked.

"Nope. Got fired. I reckon the gal ain't got no ear fer music."

"Is that what she said?"

"Nope. She jest allowed as how her and the Enright polecat had figured my kinda talent might be appreciated better over here. Sorta snappy about it, she was."

Sheldon frowned. "I wouldn't have expected that kind of pettiness from her."

"I got a feelin' Enright prodded her into it, Ross. He's been actin' mighty uppity around the camp today."

"No matter," Sheldon told him. "We'll find a job for you — even with the banjo. No hurry, I suppose?"

"Nope. She gimme a extry ten dollars when she paid me off."

"Conscience money, I suppose."

"Mebbe not," Smoke said innocently. "It could be extry pay fer music."

Sheldon laughed. "She might pay you ten dollars to get . . . but never mind. Throw your kit in that third wagon and tell Baldy he's got company for supper."

He was about to turn to something else when a tall, well-built man in uniform came around the end of the storage sheds. His stride was suggestive of youth but the drooping mustache that half-concealed his smile was as gray as the shaggy hair which showed beneath the flat garrison cap. Sheldon stared in surprise for a moment then hurried to meet him, hand outstretched.

"How are you, Rowdy?" he greeted. "I didn't have any idea you'd still be out here."

"I didn't plan on staying," his visitor told him. "But things happen to make a man change his mind."

Sheldon nodded. "It's sort of a shock to see Colonel Rowdy Russell of the Seventh Iowa Cavalry wearing a lieutenant's uniform. Is that the best they'd do for you?"

"Seems so. The army was lousy with officers and everybody took some kind of a cut, even the regulars. There's plenty of companies commanded by brevet-brigadiers and colonels. I suppose I was lucky they even let me get a regular commission. But what about yourself? I thought you'd be a lawyer by this time."

"Like you said. A man changes his plans sometimes."

"The girl? The one you used to talk about — Alice?"

"Partly. She didn't seem to be impressed with my war record. Some of the other boys were coming back from the lower Mississippi or Virginia with medals and commissions — and wounds — but I was just a fellow in dirty clothes who'd watched the war from a nice seat in the balcony."

"Forget it," Russell said quickly. "When I heard you'd arrived at the post I thought of something. Last fall you promised Louis Gazzous a couple of loads of potatoes. I had a hunch you'd remember your promise."

"I promised to send 'em by the first train west. Since I brought almost the first one — something I didn't plan on when I made the promise to Louis — I made his spuds part of my load. What's that got to do with you?"

"Are you taking the potatoes up yourself?"

"I figured on it."

"Then you can do something for me. My command just now is a scout company. With the peace conference gathering it's considered to be bad strategy to send troops of any kind out on patrols of any sort but we need to know a bit more than we do about some things. That's where you come in. You can get more out of French Pete than a patrol could get by observing the country for a month."

"Sounds easy enough. What kind of information do you want?"

"Anything that will help us to outguess the intentions of the Indians. These peace commissioners are a lot of idiots. They expect us to supply them with presents of arms and ammunition — for the red brothers to use in hunting, of course — and they insist that we make no moves that will seem at all warlike. If they succeed in making a deal with the Sioux that will work out, all right; but some of us don't think they're going to make the deal. Meanwhile we're going blind in the face of a powerful enemy. That's foolishness."

"Any reason to think the peace talks will fail?"

"Ask yourself. You spent enough time out here to know something of the Indian mind. You know that Indians don't make much fuss about a few trappers or traders but they don't want whites piling into their country wholesale. The Bozeman will flood their best hunting ground with all kinds of people. They won't stand for it."

"Sounds reasonable. Sam Hanna stopped with us the other night and he talked the same way."

"Then you know about Carrington. Good. We need information for him as well as for ourselves. He'll have the same handicap we have."

"I'll see what I can learn. Come along and have supper with us."

Russell accepted the invitation promptly and they went across to join Cope and Prine. Greetings were informal all around. The Iowa Cavalry had never been strong on discipline and Colonel Russell had been Rowdy to almost every man in his command. That he now wore the uniform of the regulars didn't alter matters at all where his old friends were concerned.

"You'll be having a visitor one of these days," Sheldon told him when the first hilarity was over. "Sam Hanna told us the government is sending some kind of agent out here to look into charges that the Indians were stirred up by Confederate agents."

"We've heard about him," Russell said dryly. "Orders came that he was to be given all possible assistance."

"Sam was asking questions for him. He seems to be interested in fellows like Crabiel and Twiss."

"That's just a part of it," Russell growled. "Some of those fire-eaters in Congress won't be satisfied until they've made somebody sweat blood for the mistakes of the past four years. They're demanding military rule of the South and they're out to punish anybody who can be accused of having anything to do with the rebellion. It's rumored that they plan to carry their vengeance into this country, hounding anybody they can accuse. That leaves a lot of men out in the open as targets, you know. We had plenty of draft-dodgers out here as well as a sprinkling of Galvanized Yankees."

"I wish you luck," Sheldon told him wryly. "You'll be just the man he'll depend on as his source of information. An agent like this one will expect you to know the names and political sympathies of every man you ever met."

"I'm afraid so. Makes a man want to take up sheepherding or something. It's bad enough to fight Indians while your own government sends out agents to supply them with arms and ammunition. Putting a political wrangle into the mess just makes it that much worse."

When Russell left the wagon camp Sheldon gave his orders for the move north. "We'll leave early tomorrow morning," he told Cope. "There's no point in delaying. While the peace talks are still peaceful ought to be just the time to get on the trail. I'll take Prine instead of Ludlam. That'll give you Eli for the Platte crossings. It'll work better that way."

No one objected. Two teams of the soundest animals were separated from the others so that they would be available in the morning.

CHAPTER
SIX

It still lacked a good hour to dawn when the two wagons rolled out of Laramie the next morning. They were well clear of the sprawling encampment when the sun climbed into view above the rolling country to the east, a condition Sheldon had considered in making the early start. It was just as well not to have their departure witnessed by too many Indians. A pair of wagons without escort might be too tempting.

They met bands of Sioux almost as soon as it broke full day, the loaded pack animals and travois indicating that whole families were coming to the peace talks. That was good. The bands of young bucks on the loose were the parties to be dreaded.

The day proved fine, Laramie Peak showing brilliantly in the sunshine from its sixty-mile distance, and the two wagons made good time. The little bands of Indians seemed to be giving the trail a wide berth and by mid-afternoon Sheldon knew why. He had begun to watch the trail a little more closely instead of keeping his gaze on the hills and ridges. The fresh sign of other wagons ahead was clear enough.

He stood up on the wagon seat and yelled back to Smoke. "Think your team can make it to Little Bitter Cottonwood?"

"I reckon," Prine shouted back. "Be most dark though."

Sheldon waved him on and sat down again. Maybe this would be the bit of luck they needed. The problem of night camp with only two wagons and two men had been bothering him most of the day but now it seemed as though the problem would have an easy solution. A train of any size would almost certainly pick Little Bitter Cottonwood for their night stop. Nowhere else within miles would they find firewood, grass and water in such abundance.

There was still a trace of red in the western sky when they saw the campfires ahead and within minutes they were being hailed by nervous guards. The train proved to be one of Mormon converts headed for Utah, many of them green Easterners who had got pretty nervous at the sight of so many bands of Indians. Their leader stated flatly that he would be glad to get through this particular piece of country and he welcomed the newcomers, particularly when he discovered that they were old hands at the business.

Next morning an extra man was assigned to drive Sheldon's wagon so that the train could have his services as guide. He led them over a by-pass to avoid the dangerous windings of the North Platte canyon and they made their night camp just above Horseshoe Creek. By that time he and Smoke were on good terms with the entire company, and that night Smoke risked their new popularity with a sample of his musical art. It wasn't much fun, Sheldon thought. Everyone was too polite about it.

Another day saw them through the strip of badlands, where everything was hot, dry and dusty. Red and yellow buttes reared ugly flat heads out of the white, powdery flats until the whole region looked like an endless succession of abandoned brickyards and old mortar beds. Sheldon remained out ahead with the train captain until the worst of the badland country was behind them, then he spoke a brief farewell and dropped back to take over his own wagon. Bridger's Ferry was just ahead.

When the train moved on westward along the south bank of the river the Sheldon wagons cut to the right and made the crossing without delay. The ferry operator, a rancher named Mills, told them that there had been several bands of outlaw Sioux in the neighborhood for a week and that they had made a couple of half-hearted attempts on his stock. He thought they were holding off for some kind of signal from the chiefs at Laramie.

Late in the afternoon they saw Indians along the river and the sight made for a nervous camp that night but they were not disturbed, moving out before daylight after scant rest for either of them. Both were riding with rifles across their laps now but still nothing happened. Sheldon wondered about what the ferryman had told them. If these bands of roving warriors were being held in check it indicated there was a pretty strong power back of their organization. Indians usually didn't take orders so well. The continued peace was beginning to seem ominous.

The next day was a repetition of the tension but again they were undisturbed, reaching the mouth of Sage Creek in the afternoon and soon seeing ahead of them the collection of slab shanties which marked the trading post of Louis Gazzous, also known as Louis Gazzons or Louis Gasseau but most commonly called French Pete.

Several Sioux warriors stood in front of the largest building, talking to a couple of white men, while around the establishment a half-dozen swarthy children, played or worked at various chores. Pete's Sioux squaw had provided him with helpers as well as with a contact for doing business with the Indians.

They drove the wagons into a side yard and Sheldon went around to the door, ignoring the hot musky smell of the Indians who crowded him on either side. Their hostility was evident but he spoke directly to one of the white men, a fellow he remembered as a trader named Arrison. "Louis around the place?"

Arrison grinned. "He's inside. Looks like ye kept yer promise. Louis was talkin' about them spuds only yestidday. We didn't figger ye was goin' to bring 'em yerself."

He led the way into the shack, explaining, "Me and Louis went pardners. Sorry ye didn't bring more stuff; we could sure use it."

The inside of the store was a lot more impressive than the outside. Canned fruits, cheese, tobacco, liquor, crackers and hardware lined two sides of the room while behind the door and along the other wall were displays of bright calico, beads, gaudy ribbons, knives and other articles calculated to appeal to the Indian. French Pete was haggling noisily with two warriors, the deal involving some newly cured wolf hides and a bolt of red cloth. Mr. Gazzous and his new partner were prepared to do business on a strictly divided basis, it seemed, their Indian stock separated from the items they expected to peddle to white emigrants.

Sheldon waited until the deal was completed, Arrison talking swiftly in low tones during the interval. His explanation made good sense. The post was being stocked as completely as possible but they were making no attempt to improve their tumbledown buildings, figuring that they would make the attempt to rebuild only if the Laramie conference turned out to be a success.

If the Bozeman was opened, this store would be the main post for the new partnership, with a branch store somewhere up along the Powder. If the Sioux refused to open the Bozeman the whole area would become too risky and the post would be moved a little farther to the west out of Sioux country. Evidently Gazzous was not figuring too optimistically on his thin relationship to the tribe.

Finally the Frenchman came across to shake hands, the excellence of his English noteworthy for a man who used two other languages by preference. There was a brief exchange of personal explanations and then they talked business. It was almost as quick a deal as the one with Bullock except that this time it was an outright sale. French Pete was not disposed to haggle over prices. Potatoes were always good for high prices in spring. People who had been on salt pork and dough all winter needed something of the sort to curb the threat of scurvy. Indians and settlers alike would pay well for potatoes; even the new emigrants would be good customers since most of them could not afford to burden their wagons with such a heavy commodity.

It was quickly agreed that Sheldon would pick up two loads of pelts which Pete had taken in trade from the Sioux, carrying them to Laramie for the Frenchman's account with Bullock and Ward. The balance, which would be in favor of the trader, would be left with Bullock after Sheldon took out his share. They each signed a memorandum and the deal was complete. Again Sheldon had the satisfaction of feeling that his move had been a good one. There had been risk in the trip but the contact with an established trader was important to a new freight company.

The Sioux rode away while the business was being handled and the post quieted down a little. Sheldon took advantage of the lull to ask the questions he had in mind, Arrison's early remarks having given him just the right opening.

"Sounds like you don't expect the Laramie talks to shape up good," he commented casually. "Arrison says you're ready to pull up stakes."

Gazzous shrugged thin shoulders, his pointed beard waggling a little as he chewed solemnly on his tobacco. "We think no," he stated. "Many white men make bad hunting. For the Sioux nothing is worse than bad hunting. They will not agree."

"All of them feel the same way?"

"Who can tell what they feel? We know only what they talk. Spotted Tail, Standing Elk and Swift Bear will talk business. They say the white man will come, no matter what they do. They say better to take pay and lose their hunting ground than to lose their hunting ground after losing many warriors first. Red Cloud and Man-Afraid-of-His-Horse say they will fight."

"So Red Cloud's talking war, is he? Will many of the young men follow him if he goes on the war path?"

Gazzous shrugged. "Who is to know? The Indian has many notions. That is why we hold ready to move in either direction."

"What about white men stirring up the Indians? There's some talk of that."

"As ever, they sell whiskey. You know what it means."

"Then the government hasn't caught up with Richards and Bissonette yet?"

Gazzous shook his head. "Richards is gone. No one knows where. Maybe to join with Major Twiss and Crabiel."

"And where are they?"

"Twiss I do not know of. Rumor is that he lives along the Tongue or the Powder, having become almost a Sioux in everything. Crabiel I have heard about from the relatives of my woman. He no longer supplies whiskey to the Indians but lives as a hermit in the Big Horns. The Indians do not like to talk about him so one supposes he is crazy. Sometimes it happens to men like him."

"Then he's not stirring up any trouble?"

"I think no. Once perhaps he did so. There are even some who believe he was sent here to do it, possibly by the government of the South. Once he had plenty of money to buy whiskey but he never sold goods in return. That was two-three years ago. Now he is crazy man, feared by many Sioux because they think he has protection of the Great Spirit. Some say that Jean Moreau, the agent of Richards, deals with him at times. I do not know. Moreau I do not like."

Sheldon let the matter drop after a few more questions. He believed that Gazzous was telling the truth. The trader was just as anxious for peace as anyone.

He was awakened during the night by heavy rain, which he knew would slow the return journey. The prospect was ominous because it was becoming apparent that this stretch of trail, as well as the country farther north, was due to become pretty unhealthy. If Red Cloud and some of the other chiefs were trying to break up the peace talks they might keep their raiding parties active, partly to shame other warriors into joining them and partly to goad the white troops into some action that would disrupt the conference by alarming other Indians. Because it seemed like such an obvious move there was all the more reason to be apprehensive about the ill-boding quiet.

His mind turned to the white renegades involved. Bissonette and Richards, along with Jean Moreau, were just up to their old tricks, selling rotgut liquor to the Indians. Theirs was a dirty game but one that was easily understood. They were simply outlaws who used sneak tactics instead of violence. Twiss and Crabiel were harder to understand. Major Twiss, a West Point graduate, had deserted to the Sioux a year earlier, apparently because he liked their way of life and because he sympathized with them as victims of white greediness. Crabiel was more of a mystery and the idea that he had come into the country as a Confederate agent trying to create a diversion for the hard-pressed armies in gray was as good a theory as any. Both Crabiel and Twiss would have to be counted slightly mad, probably of no importance in the new threat of war.

It was still raining lightly at dawn but Sheldon did not mind. After the fast trip up from Laramie the mules needed the rest. Better to let them have a day than to send them out on a muddy trail. When the rain let up during breakfast time they set themselves to the job of unloading potatoes and loading furs but they didn't hurry. Sheldon wanted to let that party of Sioux warriors get well along toward Laramie before he put his wagons on the trail.

The delay proved useful, as a train of eight quartermaster wagons came in from Fort Connor at dusk. They were empty, heading toward Laramie to pick up rations, but they were in no hurry and were agreeable to having company. Sheldon grinned at Prine when they went into camp with the soldiers for the night. "Luck still with us. It was a fool trick to come up here with just two wagons but if a man has to be a fool he might as well be lucky."

"Don't sound like yer reg'lar line o' talk," Smoke chuckled. "Most times ye're gripin' about how everything goes wrong with yer plans. Now ye say yer plans were wrong but ye got lucky. What's the idee?"

"Forget it." Sheldon laughed. "I talk too much. But I guess you're right. All the things I planned so carefully seemed to break up in my fingers. I make this trip with the worst kind of judgment, taking big risks, and it all goes good. From now on I ought to blunder all the time."

The thought annoyed him all the way back to Laramie. He knew that the summary was not entirely accurate but it was close enough to the truth to be uncomfortable. Some of that smartness Winthrop had credited him with had been luck.

They arrived at Laramie in the middle of a noisy thunderstorm but even through the veil of rain they could see that the Indian encampment had grown enormously. There were also several emigrant trains along the river and it seemed clear that the peace talks had brought a great boom to the post.

Sheldon left Smoke to stay with the wagons while he went into Bullock's store to arrange for the handling of the furs. To his surprise Bullock motioned quickly for him to go through into an inner room. There was an urgency in the gesture which made Sheldon decide not to ask questions. The only customers in the place were a couple of wrinkled old Indians but he had to assume that Bullock knew what he was about. So he followed orders.

The Virginian came back quickly, asking in a low voice, "Where'd yo' leave yo' wagons, suh?"

"In your yard. Had a couple of loads of pelts to bring back for Pete. They'd better be put under lock and key tonight."

"Ah'll take care of it. Theah's a mite of trouble on hand and Ah'm supposed to keep yo' heah until Lieutenant Russell can talk to yo'." He smiled thinly and added, "The gentleman's exact words, Ah believe, were 'Tell him to stay put and don't be a fool!'"

"What's up?" Sheldon asked, frowning.

"Ah've sent foah the lieutenant. He'll tell yo' all about it but in the meantime Ah can say it's this Captain Pierce."

"Pierce? Never heard of him."

"Russell said yo'd know about him. The special agent the gov'ment sent out to investigate the ridiculous claims that South'n agents stirred up the Sioux."

"Maybe they're not so ridiculous," Sheldon said soberly. "I keep hearing a lot of rumors."

Bullock smiled faintly. "Ah'm biased, suh. As a fo'meh Vuhginian Ah find mahself under suspicion."

"That's pretty silly," Sheldon said. "You were out here long before the fuss started. Nobody had any better reputation during the war years."

"Thank yo', suh. Ah counted on yo' sympathy, seein' as how yo' seem to be on the same blacklist. That's why the lieutenant wanted yo' to stay out of sight until he had a talk with yo'."

72

"Blacklist!" Sheldon exclaimed. "What . . ."

"Lieutenant Russell can explain bettah than Ah can. Make yo'self at home while we wait fo' him."

CHAPTER
SEVEN

Bullock refused to discuss the matter further but talked freely about other matters, particularly business concerns that were of mutual interest. He reported that Baldy Cope had departed with loaded wagons on the second of June. That would put the train a full week to the east, well on its way to the Julesburg crossing. With any luck they would be back at Laramie well before the end of the summer, their westward haul having been already arranged for. They would bring back a full load of trade goods at Bullock's order.

That part was excellent but Bullock was less cheerful about the progress of the peace talks. The Indian commissioners still insisted that they had the whole show under control and that a real settlement would be made. However, the reported approach of Colonel Carrington's column had started a show of restlessness among the Oglalas and experienced frontiersmen were afraid that there would be an explosion of some sort. There were some three thousand Indians surrounding a decrepit fort manned by four companies. The little handful of whites in and around the post would scarcely know what hit them.

"Where's Carrington now?" Sheldon asked.

"We don't know exactly. Captain Pierce came in two days ago with a dispatch rider. He claimed that he'd saved a week by leaving the regiment, so yo' can make yo' own guess."

Russell stamped in then, shaking the rain from his slicker and spreading it across a chair back. "How much did he tell you?" he asked abruptly.

"Practically nothing," Sheldon replied with a wry smile. "Only that he and I are on some fool kind of suspect list. What kind of idiot did the government send out here this time?"

Russell wiped the drops from his gray mustache. "Same kind they always send," he growled. "Only fancier and more active. This time we drew a breezy young shyster who got himself a commission in the provost's department. He's a full captain, now assigned to this special investigation. He's critical of our lack of formal discipline, of our scarecrow uniforms — and of the way we do our job. We thought the Indian commissioners were the worst pests we had out here but this fellow beats them all hollow!"

He broke off to ask, "What'd you learn from French Pete?"

"Not much. Nothing on our renegades except that they think Crabiel has gone crazy and is living as a sort of hermit up in the Big Horns. Pete thinks that Red Cloud and Man-Afraid-of-His-Horse will make trouble. Maybe a couple of others but those two are the big ones to watch."

"That's the way it shapes up around here. Now let me tell you about this Pierce varmint. He showed up

75

here a couple o' days ago and made a big point of presenting his papers to the commandant. The orders are mighty definite; we're to help him in any way he demands — and 'demands' seems to be the word. Like I said, he's a lawyer, and he's going about his job as though he proposed to get indictments against everybody he can make any kind of case against."

"What's his holler against me?"

"Let me tell it my way. The first day he arrived he went right over to the Indian commissioners and got them to put him in touch with all of the red rascals that could talk English. I understand that he also spent a lot of time with this Enright feller you hauled out here."

"Where does Enright get into it?"

"Enright walked out on the Winthrop job the day you left for Pete's. He spent all his time among the Indians and the traders, asking questions. I'm beginning to think maybe he was some kind of confidential snooper for Pierce because when Pierce got into action it didn't take him long to get real chummy with Enright. Anyway, it seems pretty certain you and I weren't on Pierce's original list but now we are. It looks like Enright . . ."

"You too! What's your particular crime?"

"No particular one. I'm just a suspect because I was out here during the war. Back East they don't think much of men who served on the frontier while the big heroes were fighting the war. They think we were draft-dodgers or outlaws or Confederate deserters. To be truthful about it, a lot of us were. But a lot more of us were ordered here in spite of our requests to get duty somewhere else. You know that — and I know it — but the boys who fought the war in Washington ballrooms don't know it!"

"You mean to put Pierce in that class?"

Russell grinned briefly. "I'm just being sore, but I wouldn't bet against it. The point is there's enough truth in the charges so that anybody who served out here is subject to some suspicion. I'm on the list because I didn't go home but stayed here with a big reduction in rank. They think there's something fishy about that; either I'm afraid to go back home or I've got a crooked graft out here that may be tied up with all of the dirty work they're so sure has been going on. When Pierce saw my company of outscourings, good scouts but not in uniform, he was sure I must be some kind of crook."

"How does my indictment read?"

Russell grinned again. "Oh, you're a bad one! In the first place your war record is full of holes. There was one stretch in 'sixty-three that you don't appear on reports for ten months."

"When I was on mail detail."

"Sure. But nobody reported. To Pierce that suggests illegal activity and absence from duty. Then you were at Fort Connor for a few months. There is strong evidence indicating that the worst activities of Milo Crabiel were in that region. Nobody seems to know where he got the whiskey that he was furnishing to the Indians and there's a suspicion that he got it with the connivance of someone at Connor. Following that period you went back East and then turned up again as part owner of a wagon train. Your back pay wouldn't have been enough for such a venture so it's suspected you used profits from your trade with Crabiel."

"I can prove the facts on that one," Sheldon snapped. "Let him conduct his inquiry in the proper places and he'll find out soon enough that I used money that was rightfully mine."

"I'm just stating the facts," Russell reminded him. "The facts that sound suspicious to Pierce. He's also making a point of the fact that you made that quick trip to French Pete's. He adds it up something like this. One: you knew he was coming out here to investigate. Two: you left here in a hurry, taking two wagons to Pete's place when the wagons might just as well have gone with one of the trains moving in that direction. It couldn't have been a profitable trip and it was a risky one. Hence you had an ulterior motive, possibly to warn your partners in crime. Three: your wagon train went east without you, an indication that your freighting business is a blind for some less reputable venture."

Sheldon nodded quietly, stifling the anger he felt. "I suppose Enright provided him with some of those neat little details."

"No doubt. The important thing is that Pierce plans to have you arrested. He thinks you're the key man in a dirty crowd and he figures to put pressure on you, hoping that you'll crack and point the finger at other malefactors like Bullock and me."

"It's not funny," Bullock growled.

"What charge can he make?" Sheldon asked.

"Suspicion of treason."

"But he can't prove a thing!"

"We know that. But think of the mess we'll have if such an arrest is made. With this Indian crisis coming to a head we'll have a mess that could be more dangerous than the idiocy of the commissioners. It would give the Indian Department another charge to aim at the army and demoralize half of the units now holding posts out here. That's why I asked Bullock to get you under cover. We can't afford to have such an arrest made or such charges made public at a time like this."

"I see the point," Sheldon said thoughtfully. "But what does it look like if I skip out? He'll just add another item to his list."

"It's a stupid list. In time we can blast it to bits — but at the moment we're handicapped. The big danger is not in what he can prove but what will be the effect on the touchy situation here if the charges become a matter of gossip. We're playing a weak hand at this point and it might be fatal to weaken it any further."

"Then you want me to get out of sight to save the army embarrassment?"

Russell frowned. "Hang it all, Ross! You make it sound as though we're trying to make you look bad. Your friends know the truth. We'll help you to put this jackanapes back in a swivel chair where he belongs but we'd like to play it our way."

"You mean you've got a plan?" He grinned a little more easily and added, "I might have known you would have. Rowdy Russell always could figure some way to beat the regulations."

"Which doesn't improve my present status as a suspect," Russell said dryly. "But that's neither here nor there. Let me explain another point. One of the things that's bothering us now is the way the peace commissioners keep making presents of arms and ammunition to the redskins. They've already drawn on our magazine for a lot of powder and ball, insisting that it'll be used only for hunting purposes. Last week they distributed three hundred infantry rifles. Now we're expecting them to demand cartridges for those weapons. They have authority to make the requisition, you know."

"Naturally." Sheldon was solemnly ironic. "Everybody has authority out here except the men who have to do the fighting."

"Right. Carrington's regiment is supposed to be close now and we want to hold that ammunition for him. A couple of the Oglalas who stand in with Red Cloud have already started asking for ammunition to fit the new guns. Our guess is they want to get everything possible for themselves before Carrington arrives. Then they'll be ready to blow off the lid."

"An uprising?"

"Of some sort. We don't think Red Cloud will try an attack on the post but he'll bust the conference wide open, pulling out his gang under circumstances that will make the others choose sides. You know what that will mean."

"I can guess. The young bucks will have to choose between the dull role and the dramatic one. Most of them will go with Red Cloud. They'll be joined by the bands that are hanging around in the hills waiting for the signal to attack."

"That's about the size of it. We'll have hostiles all around, well armed and provisioned by the Indian Department. If Red Cloud plays his cards well — and he's a sharp one — he'll try to make the commissioners force our hand. Then the Indians will have most of the spare ammunition that Carrington will need so badly."

"What's all this got to do with me?"

"I'm getting around to that. Tonight I'm due to get an urgent message from Fort Connor that they're badly in need of rifle ammunition and that the Indians have been demonstrating around them. General Dandy, the quartermaster, will conveniently be absent when the message arrives and I'll assume responsibility for meeting that emergency demand. We don't have any army wagons available for the shipment so we'll hire a civilian contractor in a hurry and get the cartridges on their way before dawn."

"Wait a minute! If this is where I come in, you'd better know that I've got only two wagons available."

Russell winked broadly. "I can't deal with you; you're a shady character. I'll have enough trouble when they start trying to track down that message I'm going to get. I can't risk a deal with a man who's about to be arrested. Winthrop will get the contract. He can supply drivers but he needs a good train captain."

Sheldon chuckled. "I suppose he saw in the stars that you're about to be confronted with this emergency?"

"He'll learn about it pretty soon now. It's just good luck that he happened to remount most of his wagon boxes today. I guess he's hauled as much timber as he needs for the present."

"Sounds like you've got it all planned," Sheldon said. "Did it just happen that Captain Pierce is absent with General Dandy?"

"He's going to be. Now get your slicker and we'll get over to the Winthrop camp. Bullock will pass the word to Smoke and get your wagons sent over. We'll need 'em — and we don't want them around here to be recognized when daylight comes tomorrow."

The storm had subsided when they left the trading post but there were still occasional flashes of lightning and they kept themselves muffled against chance recognition as they splashed through the puddles toward the Winthrop establishment. Even in the darkness Sheldon could see that a row of new buildings had already gone up, some of them yet unroofed but all indicating plenty of energy on the part of someone.

He calculated swiftly. The first lot of wagons had arrived on the twenty-eighth of May. Winthrop and the others couldn't have reached Laramie before the fourth or fifth of June. And Enright had deserted almost at once. It began to look as though Harriet Winthrop had displayed a remarkable knack for getting things done.

Russell led the way to a wagon where a light showed through canvas sides, calling a discreet "Are you there, Winthrop?"

An equally cautious voice invited them to enter and they climbed in, finding the wagon box equipped as a sort of office. Winthrop occupied a chair while his daughter sat on a packing box. Both were dressed in rough clothing that showed the stains of toil but both looked brown and healthy. It seemed to Sheldon that the girl was much prettier in such garb. The lamplight brought out a tinge of bronze in the chestnut hair and a light of excitement did almost the same thing for her eyes. She nodded pleasantly enough as he entered but did not speak.

"Looks like we're going to pull it off," Russell stated abruptly. "Sheldon agrees to handle the job. I'll leave it to the pair of you to work out your own agreement on the business end. Just have the wagons at the south gate at midnight. Make sure all of your men go armed. Our escort will be a small one and every man must figure to take care of himself. Anything else you need me to explain?"

Winthrop shook his head. "I think we're clear. If we come up with any new questions we'll ask them at the fort."

"Good. Keep everything quiet but move promptly. We can't have any slips."

He went out and Sheldon grinned crookedly at the stout man. "You didn't expect to get tangled up in smuggling, did you?" he said wryly. "That's what comes of dealing with unsavory characters like Sheldon and Russell."

"I keep wondering if this isn't a mistake," Winthrop said dubiously. "I don't want to get mixed up in anything illegal — but I do believe Lieutenant Russell is doing the right thing."

He was obviously asking for moral support so Sheldon gave it to him. "It's a mess," he agreed, "but without the opening of the Bozeman Trail our fine plans for Laramie as a railroad junction won't mean a thing. I'm betting that Carrington is our best chance of getting the trail open so I suppose we ought to do what we can to help. It gives us a nice opening for army contracts."

"That's the way I look at it. There's a rumor now that the railroad won't come through Laramie but will follow the South Platte. If that's the case we'll have to change plans, but meanwhile there's business to be done with the Carrington army. His orders are to rebuild Fort Connor — changing the name to Fort Reno — and to construct two other forts on the Powder. He's bringing some seven hundred men with him — the Second Battalion of the Eighteenth Infantry — and a large baggage train with all kinds of building materials. That means a lot of mouths to feed. There'll be a lot of contract supplies sent to him before the job is done and I see no reason why we shouldn't make a try for the business."

"I like that plural," Sheldon told him with a smile. "Were you thinking of a partnership deal?"

Winthrop nodded. "That was what I told you weeks ago. I still think we can do each other a lot of good. This particular contract has to be in my name, I understand, but privately we can undertake to make it a partnership matter. Russell needed ten wagons. I could

84

get only eight ready for use, so we'll need your two. What's your idea of a proper way to split such a proposition?"

"Let's put it up to Miss Winthrop," Sheldon proposed. "She's biased, I suppose, but she's fair in her judgments. By this time she knows what a captain is worth to a train. I'll accept her decision."

Winthrop looked faintly startled but gave his consent. "It's all right with me," he said.

CHAPTER
EIGHT

Sheldon was a bit surprised when the girl accepted the challenge. He had put her in an awkward position but she didn't hesitate. Looking up calmly, she said, "Fifteen per cent to the train captain, five per cent for making the contract, wagons pro rata the balance. I'm sure Captain Sheldon will be well worth his percentage."

"Thanks. The Winthrop five per cent was pretty easy money but I won't object. The terms are the usual ones. What kind of deal does the army make?"

"Per diem," Miss Winthrop told him. "Payment for every day the wagons are gone from this post. The commander at Fort Connor may use them for a return load but only with military escort. Lieutenant Russell put that into the contract — which we will sign this evening when the emergency arises."

Sheldon chuckled at the way she acknowledged the eccentricities of the deal. "Sounds all right. Let's call it done."

They settled the various details in short order, even making arrangements for Winthrop to take charge of Cope's wagons as soon as the Bullock contract was completed. If Baldy agreed, the partnership would be extended to include other property of both outfits so as to provide wagons for some of those anticipated supply trips to the proposed new forts.

"I hope we're not being too cheerful about this," Sheldon commented, his smile slightly awry. "We plan as though nothing will interfere. Let's not forget we've got the Indian Department, the War Department, the Sioux, the Arapahoes and Northern Cheyennes all against us."

"I'm still going to be optimistic," Winthrop told him. "I'll gamble that you and Russell will find ways of making things work out. However, it's good business to draw up written memoranda of agreements like ours, so we'd better do it. Might save arguments later."

"You'll have to keep it shady," Sheldon warned him. "Pierce is not to find out that the Winthrop contract has anything to do with me. Russell would be in a mess if the facts came out."

"I've drawn up a statement of the facts you agreed upon," Harriet Winthrop said quietly. "I did it while you were settling those last points. If it reads correctly you could both sign it and we'll put it out of sight for the present."

Sheldon gave her a quick grin. "Efficient, aren't you? Must be you're trying to earn your side's five per cent. Incidentally, I had a look at the progress around here and I'd say you've been earning better than five per cent since I saw you last. That was a fast job of getting sheds put up."

Winthrop beamed with pride. "I had to eat crow," he admitted. "I sent Enright out here with the first lot of wagons because I was afraid a girl couldn't handle the job of getting things ready. Enright promptly deserted — and Harriet did everything I expected and a lot more."

The girl handed the memorandum to Sheldon. "Sign at the bottom if it sounds correct in all details. While we're passing out compliments I want to thank you for the tip about using the wagon boxes. It saved days."

There was a silence while both men read the agreement and signed it. Then they shook hands all around, celebrating the new partnership. Miss Winthrop winced a little when Sheldon grasped the somewhat grimy fist she extended. He turned it over to stare wonderingly at a fine crop of half-healed blisters.

"Chopping or digging?" he inquired.

"Both," she replied. "I like to set a good example."

"Don't do it. Out here men will work better for a lady than they will for a squaw."

She pulled the hand away. "Is that another of your . . ."

"Don't blow up! That's good advice. If you're going to be boss here, then be boss. Let the hired hands do the work. They expect it. Stick to your supervising and they'll respect you more — and you'll get more done."

Her indignation faded. "I suppose you're right. Generally you are — even if you do manage to be so annoying with it."

"That's the defect in my character," he said. "Because I'm right all the time I have to be rude so as not to be too perfect. It would get monotonous."

"A perverted sense of humor can get monotonous as well," she retorted.

"Stop it!" Winthrop ordered. "Both of you show good sense in most things but when you get near each other you act like children!"

"Spoiled brats," Sheldon corrected, shooting a meaningful glance at his flushed opponent. "But I'll relieve the situation. Time I got out there and had a look at my crew."

"McLarnin's in charge," Winthrop told him. "I knew you trusted him. He picked his own men, drivers who could keep quiet about things. I told him to save a place for Prine."

"Good. I'm glad Smoke's not on the Winthrop blacklist."

Winthrop frowned in obvious perplexity but Sheldon did not explain. He saw that the girl was staring straight at the canvas wall of the wagon. Evidently she had not told her father about firing Prine. Apparently she didn't care to admit her errors. Sheldon remembered that she had kept pretty quiet about the incident along the Platte. He backed out of the wagon in a hurry and walked away with a smile on his lips. For the first time he thought he understood something of her character. She was so determined to impress her father with her ability and efficiency that she was trying too hard. It betrayed a rather human and almost juvenile trait. Somehow he liked her the better for it.

He found Smoke with the others, the teams having already been selected and the wagons placed in readiness. McLarnin had held his picked crew together, partly for secrecy and partly to have them in readiness when the "emergency" should be announced. Old Jesse and a driver named Zane were the only ones Sheldon had met before, the others having been with the second lot of Winthrop wagons. He didn't question their selection nor make any changes in the orders McLarnin had issued.

They managed to snatch a couple of hours of sleep and then Winthrop routed them out to announce that he had just contracted to send ten wagons on an emergency errand for the army. They moved out with as little noise as possible and almost on the stroke of midnight filed in through the south gate of the decaying palisade, a sentry guiding them to the magazine.

The loading was done by soldiers of the garrison, Russell taking Sheldon aside to report. "Everything worked out fine. I'm taking a squadron out to circle west and meet you at Nine Mile Ranch. Officially it will be a routine patrol for us but we'll figure to escort you as far as the upper reaches of Sage Creek. By that time we'll know whether we need to stretch the orders and take you the rest of the way."

"Real convenient," Sheldon murmured. "You'll be gone quite a time before Pierce can ask you any questions."

"Not long enough," Russell growled. "I hope I can think of some good answers during that interval. It's getting so a man has to be a natural-born swindler to protect himself from his own side. The government sends men out to give the Indians guns. Then they send more men out to take those same guns away from the

Indians — and get shot in the process. Then they send more men out to find out why everybody is doing whatever they are doing. Maybe old Tom Twiss knew what he was doing when he went to live with the Sioux. At least he knows which side he's on now."

It was a little past one when Russell's men rode out to the west. Ten minutes later the wagons rolled northward through the darkened town. No one seemed awake to watch them go, although shouts from along the river told that somewhere someone was still celebrating the boom times. Sheldon was glad to have the buildings drop behind. It relieved the tension a little to be in the open country, although there was still no reason to relax. They were still flouting a dozen regulations and moving into hostile country.

The first pink streaks of dawn were showing when they reached Nine Mile Ranch and found the scout detachment waiting for them. Feeling fairly safe from immediate interference they stopped for a quick breakfast.

"Got clean away," Russell grinned as he hunkered down beside Sheldon to sip coffee from a tin cup. "With any luck Pierce won't get wind of it for another twelve hours or so."

"I'll feel better when we reach Fort Connor," Sheldon said. "All night I kept thinking about what it would mean to be picked up by the War Department or the Indian Bureau — or some of Red Cloud's Oglalas."

"Why don't you worry right?" Russell asked, lips twitching behind the gray mustache. "Think what it'd be like to have lightning strike one of these wagons. In case you don't know it you're hauling bulk powder and canister as well as rifle ammunition."

They had the trail to themselves as they pushed on, halting early to avoid exhausting animals that had been in harness since midnight. There was no hurry now, and the early halt gave Russell's patrols a chance to scour the neighboring ridges for Indian sign. They reported everything peaceful.

Sheldon still insisted on corraling the wagons. Ten of them made a rather thin ring so they left gaps and stretched ropes to complete the corral. It did not make for a strong defensive position but it would reduce the risk of having a sudden raid cause a stampede of stock.

The night and the following day passed without incident but all precautions continued. Not an Indian had been seen by any of the patrols and Russell came to the conclusion that the hostiles had moved closer to Laramie, waiting for some word from the chiefs there. A dozen times men quoted the famous Jim Bridger classic about looking out for Indian trouble when no Indians were in sight but the apprehensions didn't materialize. The second night passed as peacefully as the first.

Peacefully, that is, if one overlooked Smoke Prine's banjo. He dug it out that evening and ran over most of his old favorites. His themes were earthy rather than philosophical and the men replied in kind, a chorus being led by a trooper named Gus whose sense of humor was a match for Smoke's. It turned out to be a hilarious if scarcely cultural evening.

The Badlands, Bridger's Ferry and the mouth of Sage Creek fell behind and there was still no Indian threat. At French Pete's Sheldon learned that there had been no Sioux in the neighborhood for several days. Gazzous and his partner didn't like the idea. Indians didn't usually behave with so much restraint. Not only were they waiting for something but they were waiting in a disciplined fashion that was ominous. Somebody they respected very much had given orders.

Still there was no excuse for Russell to exceed his scouting orders. At the head of Sage Creek he would have to turn back. There was no point in getting himself into any more trouble than his earlier activities had already risked. The road to Fort Connor seemed safe, teamsters and soldiers, alike showing high spirits at the success to date.

That evening Smoke celebrated the occasion with a new verse. As he limbered up his banjo Sheldon noticed that Gus and his fellow troopers were getting together, so it seemed likely that a special chorus had been prepared.

Prine paid no attention. He simply launched into a verse that was the nearest thing to the original "Oh Susannah" that Sheldon had ever heard him attempt.

I had a dream the other night when everything was
   still.
I dreamt I seen a million Sioux
Come swarmin' down the hill.
Their tommyhawks was in their hands, their
   screechin' filled the plain.

I killed 'em with my forty-four
And saved the wagon train.

The chorus was ready. A dozen voices yelled out the words while the others, not in on the rehearsal, sat back and laughed.

So long, Smokey. You're the boy fer me.
We'll trust to you to skeer the Sioux
By singin' loud off-key.

They liked it so well that they repeated it, this time being joined by everyone within hearing. Sheldon hoped the good humor was not premature. He kept remembering that Fort Connor was still eighty-odd miles away.

The train moved north without escort shortly after daybreak, camping that night along the South Fork of the Cheyenne. Another night found them a short distance beyond Wind River, still with no sign of trouble. At noon of the following day they met a patrol out of Fort Connor and the mild nervousness relaxed again. Their new escort agreed to stay with them, reporting that there were no war parties in the region.

After that it was easy. Another night put them on the Dry Fork of the Powder and the next day they used the bed of the stream as their road, bumping along to the tumbledown fortification that was Fort Connor.

Sheldon was prepared to play stupid over the sending of the unneeded ammunition but he soon found that it wasn't necessary. Nobody asked questions. The disgruntled Michiganders who garrisoned the post were long overdue for discharge and they didn't care about anything except their anticipated relief by Carrington. They assumed what was actually the truth, that the ammunition was intended for Carrington, and simply made room for the wagons within the walls.

A full week of waiting followed. At first Sheldon was curious to see how the place had changed since his brief spell of duty there but he learned quickly that the only changes were for the worse. The place was being allowed to fall apart. He didn't like the look of it but forced himself to remember that it was no longer any of his business. He was just a contractor drawing daily credits on a contract while his mules rested and foraged. For the present he didn't even need to worry about the crazy charges being considered by that Pierce idiot.

Three days after the arrival of the ammunition wagons three emigrant trains appeared. They had been permitted to leave Laramie on condition that they would wait at Connor for Carrington's column to escort them through the Powder River country. Their leaders were highly scornful of the precaution. They hadn't seen an Indian since leaving Laramie and they were confident the peace talks would open the whole country without further trouble.

Two days after that a dispatch rider came in with a different story. He had left Laramie a day after Carrington's army passed the post and had been chased by Indians four times. He reported that Red

Cloud had walked out on the conference, virtually declaring war against the white man who sent one group of agents to talk peace while another group of soldiers came to take the land by force. Carrington's column was only a day or so behind him, its flankers threatened constantly by raiding parties.

The rider also brought a message addressed to "D. McLarnin, Esq. In charge of H. J. Winthrop wagons."

McLarnin handed it over to Sheldon with a grimace. "Likely fer you, Ross. I can't read writin', you know. Matter of fact, I can't even read readin'."

Sheldon ripped it open and glanced at the contents. It had no salutation and no signature. He read it aloud. "Red Cloud on the warpath. Missing renegade suspected of inciting him. Trust Brown."

"What's all that?" Smoke cut in.

"A warning to me from Russell. I seem to have made another wrong move. That jackass of an investigator is doing arithmetic again. He adds up two and two to make six."

"Better spell that out," Smoke advised. "I don't ketch on."

"Pierce thinks I've been mixed up with half of the Indian troubles west of Kansas City. He figures I went to French Pete's with some kind of dirty work in mind. So far as he knows, I didn't go back to Laramie. Then Red Cloud busted loose. That's enough for Shyster Pierce. To him it all adds up. Renegade Sheldon is back of the new trouble. I'm almost flattered that he credits me with so much energy and influence."

"But who's Brown?" McLarnin asked.

"Never heard of him. I hope he's as good a schemer as Russell. I'm going to need somebody like that."

He tried to make it sound flippant but he couldn't feel that way. The threatened Indian war had undoubtedly broken out and he was squarely in the middle of it — in more ways than one. A fortnight ago he had thought himself well on the way to being a business success. Now . . .

CHAPTER
NINE

Carrington's little army arrived on the twenty-eighth of June. There was an impressive train of wagons trailed by a long line of pack mules, the crawling column guarded by mounted infantrymen, who made a somewhat ridiculous appearance with their long rifles jutting out at awkward angles. Sheldon knew there had been talk of detailing at least one company of cavalry to join Carrington's infantrymen but apparently the planners of the movement had been as careless with detail as they had been with their timing.

Sheldon and the others watched through the waning hours of the afternoon as the newcomers made camp in the valley of the Dry Fork, keeping discreetly out of sight when officers came up to the fort. There was always a chance that Pierce had overtaken the train to press his investigations in this area and there was no point to hunting for trouble. McLarnin remained with the wagons as their official captain while Sheldon went into hiding. It was a role he hated but the general arrangement suited Prine very well; it left him to wander through the camps and gather gossip.

Shortly after noon on the following day Smoke came in to where Sheldon was restlessly waiting. His report was good. Carrington's chief quartermaster, a Captain Brown, had visited the Winthrop wagons and identified himself as the Brown mentioned in Russell's message.

Sheldon went to meet him at once, liking what he saw. Brown was a stocky fellow of about Sheldon's age, cleanshaven and with a rosy complexion that made his quick smile seem all the more boyish. He greeted Sheldon with a show of real cordiality and plunged at once into the business at hand.

"Rowdy told me the whole yarn," he said. "He was a little uneasy at giving your secret to anybody but he decided to trust me, knowing that I'm the same kind of nose-tweaker that he is. Both of us like to make trouble for the brass-button polishers. Anyway, I'm quartermaster and I had to see you about hiring your wagons to go along with us and haul that ammunition."

"What can you tell me about Pierce?" Sheldon asked.

Brown grinned amiably. "He was scuttling around Laramie like a blind badger, trying to run down all of the reports that kept coming in. My guess is that Russell invented most of the reports. I sent in a couple myself."

"Then he's not coming up this way?"

"Not right away. When he does he'll have to fight his way; the Sioux are out in force behind us."

"By the time he gets his facts together there ought to be trains moving, under escort if necessary."

"Probably. He may decide to come up this way. If he does we'll lead him a merry chase. Now about those wagons of yours. We want the ammunition along with the train. We don't have wagons to haul it. Will you bring it just as it's loaded?"

"Our contract doesn't call for that service."

"Contracts are my business. Suppose we draw up a new one, effective at once? Your wagons to be a part of whatever movement Colonel Carrington may order. Usual per diem terms. All right with you?"

"Suits us fine. Our business is to keep our wagons earning a profit."

"I'll get the contracts drawn up this afternoon. By the way, Russell said to warn you that Enright had disappeared. Maybe he's coming up this way."

"I'll keep my eyes open," Sheldon promised. "And thanks for taking an interest."

A sudden shout of "Indians" broke up the talk and everyone rushed to see what was happening. On the low hills across the river, hard-riding Sioux were driving a small horse herd ahead of them and firing rifles at the patch of timber they had just cleared. No one was pursuing them but an occasional shot from the creek bed indicated that guards were firing.

"The nerve of the devils!" Brown exploded. "Not more than a dozen of them, and in broad daylight!"

A blare of bugles from several separate points brought men running and there was a general confusion as horses were saddled. Just as the raiders disappeared over a ridge in the direction of Pumpkin Buttes the pursuit formed, some eighty infantrymen on half-controlled horses following a pair of officers.

"Major Haymond and Lieutenant Adair," Brown muttered. "I hope they don't get rash. That's not cavalry they're leading."

"What happened to your cavalry?" Sheldon asked. "I thought you were to get some."

Brown swore. "The Department of the Platte decided this is not an offensive campaign but a fort-building expedition. All we need is infantry because all we need to do is defend the forts."

Sheldon smiled sympathetically. "I see Colonel Carrington is trying to remedy the lack."

"He does what he can. At that he had to practically steal those cavalry horses. But you can't make a trooper out of a foot-slogger just by putting him on a horse. He's neither trained nor armed for that kind of work. I'll lay odds that Haymond doesn't catch a single Indian."

Guards were doubled that night but there was no alarm. Neither did Major Haymond's column return. Strong patrols pushed out at dawn, while the routine work which had begun on the previous afternoon was continued by the men left in camp. Stores had to be checked and reloaded, the Michigan men had to be relieved and sent off to Laramie, wagons had to be repaired, and the post had to be strengthened before Carrington could move on to the north.

Sheldon and Brown fixed up their contract and the ammunition wagons were moved down to a new position adjacent to the mounted infantry's camp. The new corral had just been completed when Haymond came back with his straggling mob of saddle-weary infantrymen. They had ridden seventy miles in twenty-four hours, never getting near enough to the fleeing Indians to fire a shot. Their only souvenir of the expedition was a broken-down pack horse which the Sioux had abandoned when it couldn't keep up.

The insignificant capture was soon the source of plenty of gossip. The pack had included some brown sugar, tobacco, calico dress-patterns, a spool of red ribbon, and a package of brass-headed nails. Here was proof enough that the Laramie Treaty was meaningless. Indians who had accepted gifts in return for their promises of peace were already on the warpath with the known hostiles.

Efforts were redoubled to make the post strong enough so that it could anchor this part of the proposed line of communications. The flimsy buildings of Fort Connor were abandoned and a new fort was started on the other side of the river, renamed Fort Reno. There the stores were inventoried and put under cover while decent defenses were built.

It was a back-breaking job. The country along that section of the Dry Fork was almost completely barren except for the timber in the bottoms and it was necessary to graze the stock over a wide area in order for the animals to get even sparse forage. That meant a strong cordon of guards, leaving only a few men for the real labor. To make matters worse a heat wave struck the country and for a full week the thermometer fell below a hundred only at night. With the mercury at a hundred and ten or better, wagon tires began to break or fall off as wood dried out. There was no charcoal for the blacksmiths to do any welding and only makeshift repairs could be made.

Still the work went on and on the sixth of July the word was passed that trains were to take newly assigned positions for the general movement. Sheldon's wagons didn't have to move so they had a good chance to watch the other units sifting around them and to exchange gossip with men from the other trains. Twice Captain Brown came to look in, passing along the official news of the camp. The most discussed item was the word from Laramie that the Indian Commissioners had made a public declaration that it was now safe for emigrants to use the Bozeman Trail.

It required two days to sort out the tangle but on the morning of the eighth the line of camps represented approximately the order in which the train would march. Immediately behind a company of mounted infantry would come the army wagons containing building tools, the families and personal effects of the officers, extra ammunition for the guard detail and part of the food supply. A contract train followed with two steam sawmills, some shingle and brick machines, a large quantity of glass and millwork, hardware, tools and harness. Sheldon's train would be next in line, marching just ahead of the two artillery detachments with their mountain howitzers.

He knew there would be seven other contract trains behind them, not to mention another thirty or forty army wagons, but he didn't let himself think about the obvious fact that there were not nearly enough troops on hand to guard such a column, particularly when so many of them had to drive wagons. He had long since come to the conclusion that the expedition was inadequate to the task at hand but he wasn't going to fret about it. His job was to boss a train of wagons.

Still it gave him an uneasy feeling to see those awkward-looking bluecoats trying to look like cavalry as they patroled the line of march. Out of the six hundred men under Carrington's command only about two hundred were the veterans they were rated as being. The ranks had been filled with green recruits from the East before the regiment moved West and the result was that three-quarters of them had known only basic infantry training.

Most of the officers had served in Grant's or Sherman's armies but they knew nothing of Indian warfare. They had innocently accepted General Sherman's bland promise that this would be a pleasant journey through interesting country and had brought their families along. Sherman had even visited them along the Platte and encouraged the women to start keeping journals and diaries so they wouldn't become bored by inactivity. That point had been discussed with some bitterness in Sheldon's hearing.

There was one change at the last minute. Hugh Kirkendall's wagons, carrying extra clothing and various equipment, were to take the lead position. They would unload as soon as the new fort site was selected, returning to Reno for other supplies which could not be taken along with the number of wagons available. When they moved up late on the afternoon of the eighth Sheldon watched them pass his camp and suddenly he got something of a shock. One of Kirkendall's drivers was Dale Enright.

Enright was handling an ox team, so he had plenty of time to look around, a situation which he was using to advantage. He was studying everything with sharp interest but when he met Sheldon's stare it was clear that he was completely surprised. His jaw sagged for an instant before he recovered his poise and waved a hand. At the same time he shouted something but the words were covered by the bawling of oxen, the curses of drivers, and the grinding squeal of iron tires on stony soil.

"Now we'll have it!" Sheldon grunted. "If Enright is the fellow who fed that line of stuff to Pierce he'll certainly get a message back to Laramie."

Smoke shook his head. "Mebbe he won't be able to do it. That mail outfit what arrived this mornin' claimed they'd been chased four times by the Sioux."

"They'll keep mail moving," Sheldon said. "That's one of the reasons they're leaving Fort Reno as strong as it is. The trail has to be kept open."

That night they learned from Captain Brown that one of the messages brought in by the much-harassed mail detail was to announce that a force planned for Carrington's aid had been withdrawn. The Laramie Treaty had made additional troops unnecessary. Now the mail guards were doing the loud talking about the stupidity of government agencies.

On the morning of the ninth the civilian scouts went out to take the lead with the mounted infantry. Sheldon knew most of them by sight but he had not met any of them during the week's wait. That was partly because he had made up his mind to stick strictly to business,

105

and partly because he didn't want any of them to be under suspicion if Captain Pierce should press the crazy charges he was considering. Jim Bridger himself was in command of the group but some of the others were almost equally noted. Brannan had been General Connor's guide a year before; Jack Stead was a fine interpreter as well as a skilled plainsman; Wheatly and Fisher were noted Indian fighters. On that score the little army was pretty well fixed.

The thermometer hanging in Sheldon's lead wagon registered a hundred and six degrees when they took their place in line and headed into the northwest. At noon it was a hundred and thirteen. Wagons had to pull out as horses, mules or oxen collapsed but the main column pushed on, covering the twenty-six miles to Crazy Woman Fork before corraling for the night.

They stayed there for three days, making the repairs which should have been made at Reno. Wood was cut and turned into charcoal so that tires could be welded, a tedious operation which occupied most of the time involved. On the morning of the thirteenth they moved again, the heat a little less vicious. Indians were in sight almost constantly as the train rolled along, and shortly after passing Rock Creek, word was passed along the line that one of the scouts had found a note left by the emigrant trains which had pulled but of Reno several days ahead of the main column. They had been attacked by a strong force of Sioux at that point but had suffered no casualties although they had lost some horses.

Again they made good time, passing the salty expanses of Lake DeSmet before going into camp on Big Piney Fork. This was the general area where the second fort was to be built, so again the trains were placed in corrals that would be of some permanency. They were now virtually in the shadows of the Big Horns and Sheldon wondered what Enright must be thinking now. If the man actually was on the trail of Milo Crabiel he had got pretty close to his destination. Crabiel was supposed to be living back there in the mountains somewhere.

That night Captain Brown came to the wagon camp. "We're going out to survey the country," he told Sheldon. "The Colonel wants to look things over carefully before he decides where to build Fort Philip Kearny. That's to be its name, you know. Want to go along?"

Sheldon hesitated. He didn't want to get involved in any activities which might be further misinterpreted but he knew it was good policy to become favorably known at headquarters. Future contracts had to be considered as well as the possibility that Pierce might turn up in the neighborhood.

Brown misconstrued his hesitation and added, "Your train won't need you while we're gone. Anyway we can use another man who knows the country."

"Then don't count on me. I've never been this far north before."

"Let's not get scientific about it," Brown said. "I wanted to go with them and I told them I knew a man who'd be valuable. Don't spoil it for me; I'm getting

107

mighty tired of doing my soldiering with account books."

Sheldon grinned crookedly. He suddenly realized that Brown was a fellow sufferer. Neither of them had drawn the assignments they wanted. "You're taking a long chance," he warned. "Linking yourself with a suspected renegade just to get an opportunity to go scouting is something of a risk."

"No risk," Brown said airily. "The Colonel knows all about you."

"What? How . . . ?"

"I told him. It was the day after you mentioned to me that you had seen your old chum Enright with Kirkendall's wagons. I got to thinking about the fellow and I had a feeling that if he was slippery enough to impress Pierce he might try the same thing with Colonel Carrington. So I gave the Colonel the whole story. We've had a sergeant keeping an eye on Enright ever since."

Sheldon's smile widened a little. "Sounds like you've been taking good care of me — and I suppose it's the smart way to handle it. Trying to stay under cover is no way to fight a thing like this. Sooner or later I've got to meet Pierce and prove to him that he was wrong. I might as well have some honest people on my side when the showdown comes."

Brown looked relieved. "I'm glad you don't feel that I violated your confidence. Then you'll go along in the morning?"

"I'll go."

"Good. In addition to Colonel Carrington and Adjutant Phisterer we'll have Brannan and Stead. Captain Ten Eyck will go along in command of a squadron of his homemade cavalry. The idea is to swing over along the base of the Big Horns to see if a better trail might be marked out. Bridger doesn't like the Bozeman so we won't build a fort along it if there's a prospect of abandoning it for a different road."

"Going to take the band?" Sheldon asked quietly.

Brown's surprise was almost funny. "The band? What'd be the point of taking the band?"

"Best-armed troops in the regiment," Sheldon said. "I watched them drill the other day. They've got the new Spencer carbines while everybody else totes a long rifle around. Ten good horsemen with those repeaters would be worth more than a full company of misplaced plowboys with their muskets."

"You're too blame smart," Brown said with a grin. "Those were the orders and the Colonel won't be persuaded that he has the authority to make any changes. Maybe you ought to mention it to him."

"Not me. I'm a renegade. If Pierce hears about it he'll figure out it's some kind of dirty plot to demoralize the regiment."

"Have it your own way," Brown agreed. "Be ready at five o'clock."

CHAPTER
TEN

Brown had scarcely left the wagon camp when another visitor arrived. Henry Arrison, partner of French Pete, rode into the corral and dismounted, exchanging greetings with several of the men he knew. Sheldon had a feeling that the trader was worried but Arrison's greeting sounded easy enough.

"I'm lookin' fer information," he announced. "Is the army goin' to build a fort here or up on Tongue River?"

"Nobody knows yet," Sheldon told him. "Colonel Carrington is going out to look things over tomorrow. We'll soon know, I suppose."

"What's he looking fer?"

Sheldon hesitated before replying. Arrison was the partner of a man who was related by marriage to the Sioux. Gazzous had always had a good reputation on the frontier but circumstances put him under suspicion.

As the phrase went through his mind he almost laughed aloud. Now he was thinking like Pierce, mentally accusing a man simply because the man had opportunity.

"He'll study the usual things, I suppose," he said finally. "The new fort will have to protect the road and it'll have to be strategically placed for that purpose. It will have to have good water, timber and graze. I don't know what else the Colonel will have in mind but he'll have to consider those points."

"That's good enough fer me," Arrison grunted. "Tongue's purty country and it's got good grass but they'd sure be in a bad way fer timber. I'll tell Pete we could figger on 'em building somewhere around here."

"Where's Pete now?"

"We got five wagons down by the crick. Been on the tail o' this army ever since it left the new fort on Dry Fork."

"Going to set up a post here?"

"Not yet. We're plannin' to travel around a bit, tradin' with the villages near here and waitin' to see how the cat's goin' to jump. Mebbe we kin take a quick profit before the trouble busts loose."

"Then you expect it?"

The worry showed again but the reply was casual enough. "Looks like it to us. Pete figgers the varmints ain't ready to start nothin' big yet. Red Cloud's hopin' he kin bluff the army out."

"Which he can't, of course."

"Sure. You and me know it. Pete knows it. But Red Cloud ain't sure. While they're makin' up their minds we oughta be able to make some fast deals by coverin' a lot o' country. We jest want to make sure we don't git too fur away from this here army."

"And you think there are a lot of villages near here?"

Arrison shrugged. "Pete figgers it that way and he oughta know. He claims they've been movin' right along with the column all the time."

"Then you'd better watch your step. They might start with you."

"Ain't likely," the trader replied. "Pete's got kin with 'em and anyhow they ain't mad at traders. What they don't want in their country is settlers and forts."

He left shortly after that and Sheldon crawled into a wagon to get some sleep. He didn't like what he had heard. The Sioux were still displaying that unusual quality he had noted weeks earlier. There had been small raids but nothing of consequence. A large force of warriors was waiting for something to happen, waiting in a manner which hinted at a lot more discipline and planning than Indians usually displayed. It didn't sound good.

The reconnaissance party went out on schedule, Sheldon riding his mule and easily keeping pace with the horses of the officers. They covered a dozen miles in almost complete silence, swinging west and then to the north along the lower slopes of the Big Horns. It was a beautiful day for such a ride, the sun bright but not too hot, the snow-covered peaks of the Big Horns offering a scene of grandeur that was in sharp contrast to the lower ridges and distant flats to the right of the party.

Within three hours it became clear there would be no point in changing the line of the road. The Bozeman Trail ran between a series of low hills and the first shoulders of the Big Horns, using fairly level ground. Any new trail to the west would be more billy and less open.

In mid-morning they halted to rest their mounts and Sheldon joined the circle of officers and scouts because it was plainly expected of him. No one had made any point of greeting him when he joined the party but all along he had been accepted as a regular member.

"We'll stick to Bozeman's trace," Carrington told them shortly. "Now we must decide whether to build the fort on one of the branches of the Powder or on the Tongue."

No one commented and he aimed a question directly at Brannan. "You've been through this country, Brannan. What's your guess?"

The scout's lean shoulders hunched expressively. "The main idea is to keep the Sioux in check. That means a fort on the Powder because that's where they mostly hang out. Clear Fork or Big Piney oughta be about right."

"Stead? How do you see it?"

The interpreter nodded. "I'll go along with Brannan."

"Sheldon?"

"I'd say Big Piney, sir. A big fort will mean lots of timber. Piney's got it. Tongue has grass but not the right kind of trees."

Carrington nodded. "That's an important point. However, we'll take a look. According to my map we're not far from Tongue valley right now."

They rode into the valley of Tongue River an hour before noon and paused just long enough to survey the pleasant grazing country from a commanding ridge. Carrington promptly ordered a return. Tongue was not the location. It would be a monumental task to bring in enough logs to build a fort here.

Brown took Sheldon aside when they halted for a noon meal. "I thought you'd never been around Tongue," he said with a frown. "How'd it happen that you knew about the shortage of good timber there? Neither Stead nor Brannan mentioned it."

Sheldon aimed a quizzical grin at him. "Don't you remember? I'm a renegade. I've been all over this country stirring up Indians and selling them bad whiskey. I also rob widows and orphans. Ask Pierce."

"Don't be a blasted fool!" Brown snapped. "That kind of talk might get back to some idiot like Pierce and you'd have more explaining to do."

"Sorry. The way you asked the question made me forget you're on the right side. The fact is that a fellow named Arrison came to see me last night just after you left. He told me that Tongue doesn't boast good timber."

"Arrison?" Brown repeated. "That's the partner of French Pete, isn't it?"

"Right. I suppose I'm all the more suspect now because Pete is high on Pierce's blacklist."

"We're keeping an eye on all traders," Brown informed him soberly. "I can tell you that two nights ago Pete's wagons camped along part of our train and your friend Enright went over to visit him. That could mean something."

"Of course it could. It probably means that Enright thought he had a chance to get a line on Milo Crabiel.

Gazzous and Crabiel were both mentioned in his hearing the night Sam Hanna brought up the subject."

"You're still taking a risk to get tied up with questionable people."

"Who isn't taking a risk out here? At the moment I've a lot more to fear from Red Cloud and his Oglalas than I have from a two-bit shyster in brass buttons."

Brown laughed aloud. "Well spoken! Let's get some coffee and drink a toast to Pierce and the Sioux. To the devil with both of them!"

On the return trip Carrington motioned for Brown and Sheldon to ride on either side of him. His first words indicated that he had made up his mind about locating the new fort.

"We'll build along Big Piney," he stated. "Tomorrow we'll lay out the site and I want every able-bodied man assigned to the work. Captain Brown, you will detail a lieutenant to the work of organizing the wagon trains and moving them into positions adjacent to the site selected. We want all tools and equipment as handy as possible. Your sergeants can handle the routine details of your regular work while you take charge of erecting the sawmills and other machinery.

"Mr. Sheldon, I understand that your wagons are under an indefinite contract to us. Are you willing to carry on that contract by putting your men, teams, and equipment to the work of hauling timber?"

"At the same rates, sir?"

"Of course."

"That would suit us fine." It was not a question to require much consideration. Returning the wagons to

115

Laramie would involve a certain amount of risk and the advanced state of the season would make future contracts something of a gamble. By staying on the timber detail the profits would be continuous and certain.

"Captain Brown will make out the supplementary contracts as soon as convenient. Dismount your wagon boxes and leave them as temporary storage boxes for the ammunition. Men will be detailed to assist at the chore. By the time the wagons are rigged for timber handling we should have the woodcutters at work and you'll be able to start bringing in loads."

When they rode into camp at six o'clock Sheldon felt reasonably satisfied with his day. He had gained recognition from the commander and he had learned that Colonel Carrington meant business. Fort Philip Kearny was going to be built — and promptly. After so much doubt and delay it was good to know that matters were now being handled by a man who could make decisions.

They found considerable excitement in the camp on Piney Fork. During the day several men had deserted, supposedly to head up the Bozeman Trail to reach the Montana gold fields. Lieutenant Adair had sent a detail in pursuit but the soldiers had been stopped by a strong force of Indians.

The Indians had already surrounded the wagons of Louis Gazzous and one of Gazzous' drivers had been sent as a messenger to the soldiers, warning them that they would not be allowed to proceed northward. There had been no attack but the intention of the Indians seemed ominous so the troopers returned to the camp, bringing the Gazzous driver with them.

Sheldon went along with the headquarters party to interview the man. Brown suggested it, mentioning that Sheldon had done business with Gazzous and might know the messenger. Oddly enough it was Brown who recognized him. The boy — and he was no more than that — had driven an army wagon from Laramie to Reno but had been discharged because of his age. He readily admitted that he had slipped away from the train that was to take him back to Laramie, getting a job with French Pete instead.

He repeated the warning the Indians had sent. The white soldiers were to retire at once from Powder River. The Indians would not molest Fort Reno or its communications but they would not permit the whites, soldier or settler, to come beyond that point. They further demanded that the white chief and Jack Stead should come to their village and bring an answer. Would it be war or peace?

Carrington questioned the boy closely but only one fact seemed to be of any significance. The Indians who had sent the warning were Cheyennes, not Sioux. Gazzous had said that the Cheyennes were trying to avoid war and that this was an honest warning. The Sioux were trying to force the Cheyennes into alliance with them but the Cheyennes were hopeful of avoiding a decision.

"You think this particular band is honestly friendly?" Carrington asked.

The youngster shrugged. "We deal with 'em. Pete thinks they're scared of the Sioux. Anyway they didn't hurt nobody."

Brown asked permission to fire a question and Carrington motioned for him to go ahead.

"Were you with Pete's wagons the other night when a man from this camp came to see him?"

"Sure. I heard 'em talkin'. It was a man name of Enright. He wanted Pete to hire him as a driver. Pete didn't need no more drivers."

"Did Pete know this man from before?"

"Didn't sound like it," the boy said, scratching his head thoughtfully. "But then, after the man left, Pete said he knew about him. Pete thought he was a crook or somethin'."

"But the man named Enright didn't ask any questions while he was there?"

"Sure he did. He wanted to know if a feller named Crabiel was livin' around here. Pete said he didn't know."

Brown sat back, shooting a glance at Sheldon. Colonel Carrington did not comment although it seemed certain that he understood the meaning of the exchange. Instead he looked at Jack Stead and asked, "Are you willing to go to the Indian village, Stead? It might be risky."

"Not if they're Cheyennes," Stead told him. "I got me a Cheyenne squaw, you know."

"Then you and the boy can take them a return offer. Invite them to come here day after tomorrow. We'll try to make some kind of terms."

118

No one was very hopeful about the prospect of an agreement but in the next forty-eight hours there was no time to think very much about it. At dawn the following morning Carrington and his aides started to lay out the site of the fort, choosing a slight elevation just back from the camp site and close enough to Big Piney Fork so that water supply would be assured. In many respects it was a weak position, being commanded by a superior elevation only a little distance to the east, but there was no chance of artillery being brought into use by an enemy and the small weakness was ignored. The important matter was that the site was relatively clear of surrounding trees. Defenders could sweep all approaches with rifle fire.

Sheldon's wagons were moved to the spot immediately after breakfast, a work detail helping with the task of removing the boxes and repacking the ammunition in them, the makeshift magazine being spotted beside the location where the permanent storage would be made.

When noon rolled around, remarkable progress had been made. Brush had been cut, the lush grass of the plateau had been mowed to form a parade ground and rows of tents were springing up where barracks would soon be built. Down by Big Piney, one sawmill was almost ready to get up steam and the second was being assembled swiftly. Even the mountain guns had been hauled up the slope to the spots where they would be mounted behind palisades. Fort Phil Kearny was going to be quite a sight for the Indian visitors to see when they arrived. Maybe they wouldn't be quite so impudent when they saw what progress the white army could make in such a short time.

The work went on during the afternoon but Sheldon took no part in it, riding out with Captain Ten Eyck and Lieutenant Wands for a survey of the available timber. An hour of scouting warned them that they wouldn't find much big material close at hand, but the general result was not too bad. An island in the creek had the finest stand of timber on it, big pines that could be sawed into fine boards or good squared timbers. It was seven miles from the fort but the timber was good enough to make the trip worth while. They recommended to Colonel Carrington that two timber details be formed, one to bring in the big trees while a second worked on smaller growth closer to the fort. The smaller trees would be good enough for minor timbers and for the palisade that was to go up.

That evening orders were issued. The entire garrison was divided into details. Woodchoppers, diggers, construction workers, mess details and guards drew their assignments, all but the guards having civilian workers with them as idle wagon drivers took on paying jobs. The hauling of timber would have to be a contract freighters' job since the army wagons were either without drivers or were badly needed for other work.

At dawn of July sixteenth the first wood train went out, Sheldon in charge of his own wagons and eight others that had been made available by the unloading of the sawmills and other equipment. The three different contractors who owned the eight additions were only too happy to have their wagons put into profitable service without delay.

Lieutenant Adair commanded the fifty-man guard detail and the train set out briskly, Sheldon riding ahead to make sure that they followed the trail previously decided upon. To avoid ambush and to find open country for the wagons they climbed to the shoulder of a low ridge which lay northwest of the new fort between Big Piney and Little Piney. Keeping to the shoulder of this chain of hills they wound around to a spot where Big Piney rushed down toward its sharp turn eastward. There was the island with the big pines, an easy ford giving access to the excellent building material.

At first the work was slow, green axemen making clumsy assaults on the towering pines, but before long the trees began to come down. Half of the guards did the chopping, trading jobs each hour to avoid too many blisters from the unaccustomed toil. The logs they loaded upon the stripped-down wagons were pretty ragged at the ends but they were logs just the same. Out of them would come the planks, sills, joists and studs that would turn a camp into a defense and a habitation. When noon arrived the train was already on its way back, guards and teamsters alike feeling the importance of the occasion. Fort Phil Kearny was on its way.

CHAPTER
ELEVEN

They made another trip in the afternoon, this one taking less time because the woodchoppers were ready with the logs when the wagons jolted across the ford to the island. There was no interference; they did not see an Indian until they returned to the camp and found some forty Cheyennes just leaving the place after a conference with Carrington and his staff.

Captain Brown came to the wagon camp during the evening, congratulated Sheldon on the work of the day and told him about the Indian visit. Black Horse and Dull Knife had made the principal speeches, agreeing that the Cheyennes wanted peace but were being pressed hard by the Sioux to join in a general war against the white soldiers. Already many warriors had gone to join in the Sioux Sun Dance that was then in progress and the chiefs wanted the white men to leave the country before trouble could start.

"I felt sorry for the poor beggars," Brown said. "They're caught right in the middle. They're afraid of the Sioux and they don't trust us. When Major Haymond came in with his four companies and the wagons that were left for repairs on Crazy Woman Fork the Indians got real nervous. They seemed to think we were trying to spring some kind of a trap on them and they didn't stay very long after that. At the same time they're afraid they'll be marked as traitors by other Indians because they came to talk to us."

"I don't like that Sun Dance business," Sheldon commented. "When they start dancing we can expect trouble."

They didn't have to wait long. Just before dawn of the following morning Major Haymond's mule herd was stampeded by warriors who had crept undetected through his picket lines. Immediate pursuit was organized and word was sent to headquarters that the captured animals had already been driven north of Big Piney and across Lodge Trail Ridge, an elevation which bordered the stream on the opposite side from the chain of hills which led to the timber island.

The wood wagons went out with extra guards, halting almost immediately as they met a courier coming in from Haymond. He passed the word that the officer had run into a trap; he was surrounded by some three hundred Sioux on Peno Creek, just north of Lodge Trail Ridge.

The train halted until orders came for them to proceed but there was a considerable delay, during which time they saw the relief column go out. Two companies of infantry and fifty mounted riflemen looked formidable enough but it was not an effective force for such a purpose. This was where those missing cavalry detachments would have come in handy.

The wood detail worked under a strain but managed to bring in a single load in mid-afternoon, not having been bothered during the operation. When they got back with the load they learned there had been a sharp fight in Peno Valley. Two soldiers had been killed and three wounded. The stolen mules had not been recovered. Most of the skirmish had been a retreating action, Haymond's men and the relief force having to fight their way all along the line until they reached Big Piney.

It was a clear-cut victory for the Sioux but a discovery made during the retreat was the most ominous news. Haymond's men had come across the looted wagons of French Pete's traveling store, six dead men lying mutilated around the wreckage. The soldiers had rescued the Sioux wife and five children of the dead trader, finding them hiding in the brush, and the woman told her story. Pete had become alarmed at the evidence of growing war fever among the Sioux and had tried to reach the protection of the fort. On the way the little company had been attacked and massacred.

"That takes Pete and Arrison off the suspect list," Sheldon commented dryly. "Pierce ought to be real disappointed."

"I ain't real pleased myself," Smoke growled. "If a feller like Pete wasn't safe it looks real bad for some of us what ain't related to the varmints."

Still the work went on. To save travel time, two block-houses were built on Piney island and the chopping detail remained there constantly, thus keeping the wagons moving all the time. For some reason the Sioux made no serious attempt to interfere with the work and for several weeks the guards rarely saw an Indian.

Elsewhere the incidents multiplied. On the nineteenth, Kirkendall's train started back to Reno for the supplies

124

that had been left there. At Crazy Woman Fork they were attacked by a strong force and went into corral. They succeeded in getting a courier back to the fort with the warning. A company of infantry with one of the mountain howitzers went to their aid and drove off the Indians.

Then it was discovered that another train had been under attack just as it was about to meet Kirkendall's wagons. This one had been on its way up from Laramie, bringing some extra officers for Carrington, and the wife and child of Lieutenant Wands. They had been informed at Laramie that the treaty was holding good and there was peace at Powder River. The "peace" that day resulted in the death of Lieutenant Daniels and one enlisted man of G Company.

Captain Brown dropped in at the wagon camp the evening after the rescued party reached Phil Kearny. "It's getting rough," he said as he settled himself beside Sheldon. "Mrs. Wands had a nasty time of it back there. She saw the bloody rascals butcher poor Daniels and chop him up. Then they took his clothes and put them on to do a dance just out of rifle range. I'd like to get a shot at some of the butchers!"

"Too bad some of those fools at Laramie can't see something of the sort," Sheldon said, his voice grim. "Let them come up here and take a look at the peace they brag about."

"Maybe one of them will," Brown told him. "Enright went with Kirkendall to Reno. This could be his chance to get a message through to Pierce about you."

"I'm not so sure he wants to. I think Enright simply saw an opportunity to use Pierce as a means of getting even with me. Now he's just interested in locating Milo Crabiel. Pierce could be a source of trouble to him."

"Maybe you're right. He's still asking questions. A band of Cheyennes stopped Kirkendall to warn him that the Sioux were lying in ambush, and Enright hustled right over to ask the Indians questions. He had to use an interpreter, so I got a report that he was asking if any of them knew the whereabouts of a crazy hermit named Crabiel."

Sheldon just grunted. For the past few weeks he had been so busy that he had rarely thought of either Pierce or Enright.

"You take it pretty calmly," Brown went on. "I'd think you'd be madder than a hornet that a fool like Pierce should be throwing mud on a good service record."

"A fine service record I had! When I got a commission I had bright dreams of fighting the rebels and winning myself a lot of promotions and medals. So they sent me out here and I spent the time riding herd on emigrants and mail coaches with only an occasional brush with a few red outlaws. I went in a lieutenant and I came out the same way. I don't suppose I have any record for Pierce to smear."

"We're a couple of frustrated heroes," Brown declared. "I started as a private but they made me a supply sergeant because I'd been in the provision business back in Ohio. I suppose that's why I got a commission, because they wanted a quartermaster who knew his groceries. I've applied for transfer a dozen times but I'm still in the grocery business. Seems like you and I have a lot in common."

In the weeks that followed Brown expressed himself several times on the same subject. He had seen political preferment advance other men who deserved nothing, in one case a young lieutenant getting brevetted Captain for "gallant service in the Atlanta campaign," when that particular officer had been secure in a Washington office during that entire period of the war. The chief cause of his ire, however, was that he couldn't get combat assignment. Brown was thirsting for adventure.

Reports continued to come in of Indian outrages to the south. A number of emigrant trains were attacked, usually with loss of stock and sometimes with loss of life. In many cases the Indians approached their victims with a show of friendship, attacking when their hosts offered them presents. Since the emigrants were still coming up from Laramie with the understanding that all was peace in the north country treachery was made easy.

No further attacks were made on Fort Phil Kearny and early in August Lieutenant Colonel Kinney was sent with two companies and a large wagon train to build a second fort on the Big Horn River, about ninety miles above the Powder. At the same time a company was detached to reinforce Fort Reno where raids had become frequent. It left Fort Phil Kearny badly undermanned and the Indians were not slow to take advantage of the fact. This time they aimed their attacks at the wood trains.

Nearly a hundred wagons were now engaged in the work of hauling timber and the seven-mile road became almost a battlefield. Almost daily there were attempts to run off stock or to attack the trains themselves, and the guard duty became a constant skirmishing.

Sheldon and his men fought and drove throughout the entire month of August without losing a mule or a stick of timber but other trains were not so fortunate or so well organized. Hundreds of head of stock were stolen and eight men were killed within a mile or so of the fort.

In September the raiders grew more bold, attacking civilian trains, the wood detail, hay contractors and even pickets. Other men were killed both in the raids and in the pursuits which followed them. Still the emigrant wagons continued to roll northward, assured by the commissioners at Laramie that the Bozeman Trail was safe for travelers.

Twice Captain Brown managed to have himself assigned to these pursuing columns and on the twenty-third of September was given command of a squadron that was being sent out to recover a herd of stolen cattle. The result was the first real victory the white army could claim. Brown and his men closed with the Indians, killed thirteen of them and brought back the cattle.

He was in high spirits when he dropped around to talk with Sheldon on the following night. "I finally had my chance," he declared, openly triumphant. "Now maybe they'll believe I'm something besides a grocery clerk."

"Ease up," Sheldon advised. "The man who gets ideas about becoming a great Indian fighter usually winds up dead. Don't push your luck."

Brown grinned. "I suppose I'm being a bit of a fool but that's the way I feel about it. One way or another I guess we taught them a lesson this time. Maybe they won't be so bold after this."

His optimism was ill founded. Next day on Piney Island Indians scalped one of the pickets, who managed to get to the block house before he died. On the day after that the entire wood camp was besieged and the Sioux were driven out only when a company went out from the fort to shell the woods with a howitzer.

Early in October Enright appeared as the driver of one of the timber wagons now working along with Sheldon's train. They passed each other without speaking on several occasions but then Enright seemed to make up his mind about something. He grinned sourly from his wagon seat and remarked, "I see they haven't jailed you yet, Sheldon. Pretty careless about renegades lately."

Sheldon forced himself to a calm reply. "It all depends on what you call a renegade. Maybe they need me to see that you don't get to Milo Crabiel before they're ready."

Three days later he was superintending the loading of his wagons when he felt a sharp pain in his upper left arm just as a gun banged from somewhere back in the timber. Several soldiers started quickly in the direction from which the gunshot had sounded, while Smoke Prine hurried over to ask, "Hit bad, Ross?"

Sheldon stared down at the bloody patch that was showing on the sleeve of his shirt, shaking his head as he replied, "Just nicked me, I guess. I can still move the arm."

By the time Smoke and McLarnin had put a bandage on the flesh wound the soldiers were back to report that the sniper had got clean away.

"More Injun skulkers, I reckon," a bearded corporal growled in a strong Southern accent. "Musta got away fast, though. One o' the men from the other wagon train was on his tail almost before we got there."

Sheldon waited until the soldiers had gone back to their posts. Then he looked meaningly at Smoke. "Enright's wagons out here now?"

"I'll take a look."

He was gone only a few minutes, reporting that Enright was sitting calmly on his wagon not three hundred yards away. "He coulda done it," Prine growled. "Now that I think of it the shot didn't sound like a rifle. It was more like a hand gun. Ye'd better keep an eye on that polecat."

Because of the many attacks a new plan was devised for moving the wood trains. Now the wagons moved in double columns, ready to form a corral at a moment's notice. It served to halt the attacks on moving trains but the skirmishing on Piney Island continued. Sheldon took little part in the work for a full week, resting and letting his wound heal. It was not a serious one but the regimental surgeon made his orders explicit. The arm was not to be used until the healing was complete.

It was during this rest interval that a wagon train arrived with food supplies for the winter. Along with it came two visitors, one expected and one completely unexpected. Sheldon didn't even know about the expected one until the following day. He was too much concerned about the arrival of Harriet Winthrop. At least he thought he recognized her. It was almost dark when the train arrived and he saw her only at a distance as she was escorted into the fort but the suspicion was enough to bother him. What did the girl mean by coming up here into such a dangerous mess?

He sent Smoke into the fort during the evening to see what he could learn but barracks gossip was still vague. The men knew that a woman had arrived but they thought she was the wife of an officer. They were more concerned with a strange officer who had made his appearance and was having a long talk with Carrington and his staff. For some reason it never occurred to Sheldon that the newcomer was the much-discussed Captain Pierce.

Early next morning, Captain Brown came out while the wood train was harnessing. "Pierce arrived last night," he said abruptly. "Did you hear?"

"No."

"Good. We've been trying to keep him quiet so I guess we succeeded. He popped in as big as life and twice as important, demanding that we arrest the man who has been causing the Indian trouble up here. That's you, of course."

"Of course. At least, somebody from Laramie admits there's trouble."

"That's what upset him so much. He'd swallowed the peace yarns and it hit him hard when the train was attacked three times." He grimaced as he added, "To do him full credit I don't think he was scared much. Just mad. He's got it in his narrow mind that the treaty would have worked if you and some other renegades hadn't prodded the tribes into breaking it."

"Tell him to go arrest Gazzous and Arrison."

"Colonel Carrington told him something like that — and more. The Colonel had a letter about you from Rowdy Russell and he was talking to Jim Bridger. He's on your side all the way."

"Then they haven't ordered out a firing squad yet?"

Brown grinned. "Not for a day or two. Meanwhile we want you to come in at ten o'clock and talk turkey to this lad. After the Colonel took some of the wind out of his sails he calmed down and sounded real decent. Maybe he'll turn out better than we figured."

There was no opportunity to discuss it further. Smoke called a quick warning and Sheldon turned to see Harriet Winthrop and a strange lieutenant coming into the wagon camp.

"I didn't get time to tell you the second bit of news," Brown muttered hastily. "The lady arrived along with Captain Pierce and she has also been asking for you. She sounded a bit annoyed. If she's your wife and you deserted her you're crazy!"

"She's my partner's daughter and *she's* crazy — for coming up here. Any idea what she wants?"

"No. But if it's me she can have me!"

"And it'd serve you right," Sheldon told him in a whisper. "You've been itching to get into a fight. This is just the girl to provide one."

They stood erect as she came to them, Brown smiling pleasantly and murmuring a polite greeting. Apparently Miss Winthrop remembered him from the previous night for she nodded vaguely in his direction.

"Excuse me, please, Captain," she said, her tones crisp and precise. "It is very important that I speak alone with Mr. Sheldon. I hope you won't mind."

Brown made a formal bow and started across to the waiting lieutenant. Sheldon called after him, "Don't go away, Captain. The next round could be yours."

CHAPTER
TWELVE

Harriet Winthrop frowned quickly as if suspecting that the remark might have reference to her, then seemed to push the thought aside. "That man Pierce is here," she told Sheldon abruptly. "I came out here to warn you as soon as I could get someone to show me the way."

"Thanks," Sheldon replied. "I'm sorry you were put to the trouble. Captain Brown has already passed the word. He thinks there will be no trouble with Pierce."

Her disappointment was clear and he added hastily, "It was still decent of you to hustle out with the warning — but you surely didn't come all the way from Laramie to do it!"

"I came to learn what had happened to my father's property. Captain Pierce joined the train at Fort Reno and I didn't learn of his errand until yesterday. No matter how badly my father's confidence had been abused by you I thought you should be warned."

Sheldon stared at her in astonishment as he digested the meaning of the words. Then he called across to Brown and the lieutenant, "No use waiting, gentlemen. This looks like the makings of a long war. I'll see that the lady gets back to the fort safely.

"Better have breakfast with me," he suggested to her before she could protest. "It's company grub and you're company. And get rid of some of that mad look before you talk to the men. They're on their way out to do company work and they'll like it better to be working for somebody who looks fairly pleasant."

"Stop talking that way! I'm here on business and you insist on treating me like a bad-tempered child!"

"That's the funny thing about you," he said mildly. "You manage to qualify in both classes. Coffee?"

For a moment he thought she would refuse the invitation but doubt was beginning to show in her eyes. She asked, "Is the train really working?"

"Of course. I wrote from Reno when we took the contract to bring the ammunition on up here. I wrote again when we took the wood contract. Every wagon has been earning a daily fee since we left Laramie."

"But we didn't receive either message."

"No wonder you've been having doubts. I knew the Indians had gobbled up some of the mail details but I didn't figure both my letters might have met the same fate."

"I seem to have made a mistake," she told him. "We had heard nothing since you left except that you had reached Fort Reno. Then Lieutenant Russell was transferred to Fort Sedgwick and we heard nothing at all. I decided to investigate."

"Suspecting I'd stolen the wagons for some criminal purpose of my own, no doubt."

She flushed. "I didn't know what to think. I had to know."

"Did your father agree to this trip?"

"He left for Kansas City early in September, with your man Cope and every wagon he could lay hands on. He wants to make a big move next spring."

"Who's in charge at Laramie?"

"Another of your men. Ludlam. He is quite capable, I'm sure."

The wood train was ready to move and Sheldon nodded toward it. "Better give the boys a howdy. They'll like it. Then we'll straighten things out."

She followed the suggestion while he put together a camp breakfast. When she returned he handed her a mess tin and sat back to see what she would say next.

She returned to the attack. "Don't you go out with the men?"

He shook his head. "I don't need to. Since I made these new contracts I'm independent. That extra five per cent, you know. I can afford to loaf."

For a moment he thought she would rise to the bait but suddenly she gave a little laugh. "That's a deliberate attempt to start a fight, Ross Sheldon! You've got plenty of bad habits — most of them aggravating — but you're not lazy. What's the truth?"

He told her about his wound, going on to explain the tense situation around the fort. "You were foolish to come up here. Colonel Carrington is already worried about the women in the fort but he's afraid to send them south. No wagon train is safe so they have to stay here."

"But at Laramie they keep telling us that . . ."

"At Laramie they seem to have a remarkable collection of blind idiots! Your train was attacked three times, I believe."

"Four times," she corrected calmly. "One time below Reno and three times between Reno and here."

"Then I don't need to say more."

"But what can be done about it?"

"I don't know. Maybe Colonel Carrington will send a strong column south with the army families. If not, you're stuck here indefinitely."

"For the winter?"

"Perhaps. But cheer up. Captain Brown is already smitten with your charms. He's the chief quartermaster, you know, and is in charge of contracts. Maybe you'll be more good to the company here than you would be at Laramie."

She dropped her mess tin and stood up, eyes flashing. "You are undoubtedly the worst boor I ever met! You're a cad and a . . ."

"Renegade?" he asked helpfully.

"You're everything nasty and obnoxious!" she flashed. Then she was hurrying away toward the gate of the palisade.

Sheldon watched her departure a bit regretfully. She was a mighty pretty girl, even when her temper was up. It was a shame to fight with her.

A few minutes before ten o'clock he went into the fort, looking around at the way the place was shaping up. The main enclosure, six hundred feet by eight hundred, was already well filled with neatly constructed, sturdy buildings. Many of them were already roofed but

137

almost all were approaching completion and he knew that he had never seen a better fort. Colonel Carrington had built well.

He reached headquarters on the stroke of ten and was sent in by an orderly. Carrington and Brown were there, talking to a tall, spruce-looking man in immaculate uniform. The introductions were courteous and Sheldon took time to study Pierce at close range. He rather liked what he saw. There was a slight air of foppishness about the man but it seemed to be largely a matter of fine clothing and oversize sideburns. His manner was decent enough and he even extended his hand with some cordiality. Evidently Brown had not exaggerated when he reported that the newcomer had been trimmed down to proper size.

"We'll get right down to business, please," Colonel Carrington said briskly. "I think we all know the situation so we won't beat around the bush. I have asked Captain Pierce to outline his charges against Sheldon and I will ask Lieutenant Sheldon to answer each charge in detail as it is made. Is that agreeable to both?"

Sheldon nodded quietly, catching a wink from Brown. Carrington had used the military title to give Sheldon a certain status. Now this meeting was being conducted by the post commander, not by an investigator. Pierce was just another officer giving testimony.

It took a long time but there were no doubts as to how Pierce was accepting the replies. At the end he was almost apologetic, explaining, "I'm afraid I was misled by a remarkable chain of coincidences."

138

"Maybe you were misled by the way those circumstances were present," Sheldon said dryly. "Dale Enright was the source, wasn't he?"

It was the first time the name had been used in the conversation and Pierce frowned. "You know about him?"

"I know a little about him. I'd like to know more. What's his game up here?"

"I know only what he told me, that he's a creditor of Milo Crabiel and that he's trying to collect a rather large debt from the man. It was our mutual interest in Crabiel that caused us to meet. It's possible that Enright deliberately made you appear to be the center of a conspiracy."

Again they went into details, Sheldon explaining not only his personal quarrel with Enright but also his feeling that there had indeed been some kind of a plot to stir up Indian trouble. He further reported his scant knowledge as to the whereabouts of the various white men suspected of having some share in the troubles.

Finally Pierce asked, "Have you ever heard that any of these men were subsidized by the Confederate government?"

"Louis Gazzous told me there was such a rumor. I understood that he picked up the idea from the Indians. You heard about Pete, I suppose?"

Pierce nodded soberly. "You believed this Pete — that's Gazzous?"

"I did. I think he was an honest trader."

"I accept your appraisal. Now what chance would I have of finding this Milo Crabiel? If he's living in the Big Horns he can't be far from this post."

Carrington intervened promptly. "I forbid any such proposal. We are virtually in a state of siege; even strong parties fall under attack."

"But that's my duty, sir. I came to find the man."

"On this post you must accept my orders, Captain. I can't allow any such risky operation. There is something I can suggest, however. We have a few Crow scouts who help to guard our communications. Sometimes they range far afield on bits of mischief that I prefer to know nothing about. I'll have the word passed that if they learn anything about Milo Crabiel you are to be informed. Then we'll talk about plans for apprehending him."

They left it that way and for a fortnight Sheldon heard nothing from Pierce. He learned that the man had volunteered for duty with the short-handed garrison and was not pressing his own interests. That was good enough.

Harriet Winthrop had found a similar answer to her own predicament. She had been refused passage back to Laramie with a train of empty wagons returning for winter provisions, so she settled down in the feminine society of the post, helping with the children and generally making herself useful as the fort girded itself for the winter.

The broiling heat of early autumn had long since been replaced by the crisp chill of the later season, the Big Horns resplendent in color that was all the more vivid against the dark background of pines. Almost daily the peaks seemed to show more white as the early snows struck the upper altitudes and work became a dogged race against the season. It was an obstacle race, with the Sioux raids growing worse each week.

Any plan Carrington might have had for evacuating the women and children was halted by this increasing boldness of the enemy. Troops could not be spared for the protection of such a move; they were already insufficient for the proper defense of the fort and its services. The wood trains could move only under strong escort and even more soldiers were needed for the protection of the mowers who had to cut hay in distant areas to bring it in for winter storage. It was all too clear that a red noose was closing around Phil Kearny.

Still there was no sign that anyone in authority understood the plight of the garrison. Reinforcement was refused; even badly needed ammunition did not arrive. It was known that Fort Laramie now had twelve companies quartered there, including the cavalry which Carrington had been promised, but no help was sent north. Four harassed and undermanned companies would have to do the best they could on their own.

November brought the first real cold but the Indians did not seem to mind it. They continued to raid, burn and murder wherever vigilance relaxed even for an instant. For Sheldon it was a busy time. He had his regular work to do and he had to keep a wary eye on Enright. Since the arrival of Pierce, Enright had stayed pretty much out of sight. If he had been the one who fired the shot at Sheldon it could not be proved any more than Pierce could accuse him of anything illegal. In comparison with the Sioux threat he didn't seem important.

So far as Sheldon was concerned he could put Harriet Winthrop into the same category. He could forget about her most of the time. He knew that she was getting plenty of attention from the officers of the garrison, Brown being given something of a race for her company by Captain Fetterman, the senior company commander. That was to be expected and he didn't think much about it.

Nor was he the only one whose life had become a mere routine of work, eat and sleep. Wagon men were using every available moment to strengthen the corrals and the barracks that had been built for them outside the main palisade. For defense they had moved the idle wagon boxes info position but there was much more to be done. Animals and men had a long winter ahead of them and preparations had to be made. For eight long weeks Smoke Prine didn't unlimber his banjo even once.

In spite of the constant vigilance there were almost daily attacks and on the sixth of December a major skirmish developed. Sheldon's wagons held off a large force of Sioux until a rescue column arrived under command of Captain Fetterman and Lieutenant Bingham. They drove the Sioux out of the timber, allowing the wagons to proceed, while another force under Colonel Carrington swept around to strike the enemy from the flank. In the course of the maneuver Lieutenant Bingham drove ahead too rapidly and was surrounded. Before Fetterman could get to his relief Bingham and Sergeant Bowers were killed and four men were wounded.

142

The Sioux had suffered greater losses but that did not keep Colonel Carrington from issuing a sharp lecture when it was over. Bingham had showed a lack of judgment as well as a heedlessness of his orders. Some of the mounted men had run away in the midst of the fight. Captain Brown had appeared on the scene without orders. The fact that Brown had helped Fetterman to rescue Bingham's force saved him from an official reprimand but Carrington did not spare the verbal lash. In the future, orders were to be followed exactly. No pursuit was to be made beyond Lodge Trail Ridge. No matter how much an officer ached to punish the impudent raiders, discretion had to be used. With the forces available only defensive action could be taken. Troopers must not be risked on reprisals which could be turned into traps.

Sheldon felt a little easier when he heard of the session. Maybe that would take some of the ambition out of Brown. A couple of days later he discovered that his hopes were vain. Brown dropped in at the wagon camp and his cheerful grin made it clear that he was still well pleased with his share in the exploit.

"Still trying to be a hero, I see," Sheldon greeted him. "Why don't you get some sense?"

Brown merely grinned. "They're making it hard for me. Before Fetterman and the other extra officers arrived I used to get a few escort assignments. Now they don't need me and I'm back to being a grocery clerk. It makes me look bad with a certain young lady and I can't have that happening."

"If you're trying to impress Miss Winthrop you'd better forget that kind of business. She's smart enough to know that the swashbuckler isn't the only important fellow in the world."

Brown shrugged, but spoke more seriously. "Funny thing about you and her. She seems to think you're a smart lad and you appear to have a lot of respect for her ability. How come you hate each other so much?"

"We don't hate each other. We just manage to irritate each other."

"Lucky for some of the rest of us," Brown laughed. "If you ever decided to get along there wouldn't be any place for anybody else."

"Meanwhile we fight," Sheldon said indifferently. "So take your opportunity. She's a good business woman. Maybe she'd appreciate a grocery clerk."

Brown grimaced good-naturedly. "I'm betting the other way," he said.

CHAPTER
THIRTEEN

The wood train went out in mid-morning on December nineteenth, everyone a little more uneasy than usual. Snow was in the air. Black clouds were piling up over the Big Horns and the bite of winter was in the wind that swept down from the peaks. It would not be many days before work would be halted. Time was growing short for the building of defenses against the Absaroka winter and the equally bitter red enemies.

The entire train of sixty-odd wagons moved as a unit, under heavy guard and ready to corral at the first sign of trouble. It slowed the work to take so many precautions but no one argued about it. Already sixty-three men had died violent deaths at the hands of Sioux raiders and none of the men on wood detail yearned to become another item on that grim list.

At Piney Island they worked swiftly, guards watching the forest and the sky with equal interest. Sheldon walked across toward the picket line, joining the bearded corporal who had been on duty with the train so many times since the suspicious shooting incident. "Ready for snow?" he asked, smiling at the way the man was rigged up in a heavy buffalo coat and a wolfskin hood.

"Might as well be," the man replied with a dry chuckle. "They tell me it gits real peert up this away."

"Colder than Mississippi?" Sheldon inquired, guessing.

The corporal chuckled again. "Alabam," he corrected. "Mebbe I shoulda gone home when I had the chance."

"Galvanized Yank?" Sheldon asked. "Don't answer if it's none of my business."

"No harm. Wasn't much to go home to so I stuck with the army. A man gits to be an awful fool sometimes."

"You've got company," Sheldon growled. "We were fools to come up here and it took some real fools to send us — fools who still won't admit that we need help. Seen any redskins?"

"Spotted a couple on top of Lodge Trail Ridge a spell back. Kind of a relief to see the real article instead of only them blasted glasses flashin' their signals. It makes a man real spooky to know the varmints are talkin' about him from the hilltops."

"They're still talking," Sheldon said grimly. "They can't use their signal mirrors on a cloudy day like this but they're still passing the word!"

A soldier called a warning then and the corporal hurried off to investigate. Sheldon saw that it was simply a case of a distant Indian scout having been spotted so he drifted across the clearing, past the blockhouses, and back to the wagons again.

They took time out for noon mess and then the train formed, the double line moving in close formation.

146

Sheldon's wagons had the lead position in the right file so he remained, with the advance guard. Flankers fanned out on all sides and the train started, crossing the ford of Big Piney and edging up along the shoulder of the chain of hills, which now was being referred to as Sullivant Hills.

There was no sign of trouble for perhaps four miles but then a rattle of gunfire sounded from somewhere back along the line of wagons. The teamsters did not wait for orders; they swung into their defense formation so swiftly that within three minutes the entire train was in a long hollow fort, every team protected by the heavy timbers of the wagon ahead of it. The pickets remained out until recalled by a bugler and then everybody waited as the firing from the rear became heavier.

They could hear the firing coming toward them but Sheldon found time to look eastward toward Pilot Hill, the elevation near the fort on which a lookout was always stationed. He could see the guard up there signaling, so he knew that the plight of the train was being reported.

Then a half-dozen mounted Indians swept along the line, some of them firing arrows from close range while better armed warriors peppered the wagons with repeating rifles. They were met by a rolling defensive fire without any appreciable result. Sheldon thought he saw an Indian falter as though hit but the fellow swung away into the cover of the thick timber along the creek bottom and disappeared. Sheldon and his drivers did not even fire their guns. There wasn't much profit in banging away at hard-riding warriors. Better to let them come into decent range. That would be the time when the shooting would have to be good.

The attack settled into a sniping fire at long range, sounds of battle rolling up and down the line as small parties of Indians tried to rush in at various points. They were just harassing tactics, Sheldon thought, but he also suspected they were feeling out the defenses, searching for a weak spot at which to launch a real thrust. Sooner or later that big attack had to come. An Indian leader maintained his prestige only when he gave his warriors something to brag about. Red Cloud could not continue to keep a thousand fighting men in the field unless they could count a few coups now and then.

Twice heavier explosions punctuated the rattle of small arms and the beleaguered wagoners knew that the fort's howitzers were taking a long-range part in the fight. Sheldon couldn't see where the shells were exploding but he hoped that the gunners knew the exact location of the train. It would be pretty awkward if those canister shells started dropping in the wrong places.

Presently a company of mounted infantry galloped into view and he heard a soldier grunt in relief, "Powell! Glad they sent somebody who knows his business."

The train started to move even before the rescue column arrived. That was part of the usual tactics. Captain Powell and his men would do the fighting; the train and its guards had to concentrate on reaching the fort.

Sheldon attended strictly to business and just before the early dusk closed down he had his wagons in position near the sawmills, forting them at that point against the chance of a night attack. Powell's men came in just as he walked across to the fort, so he swung to the right, passing the stables where the men were unsaddling. The troops had suffered no casualties this time but the talk was pretty excited. Several hundred Indians were reported to have been engaged in the fight and other hundreds had been seen beyond the ridge.

"Lucky fer us we had orders not to cross the ridge," a burly sergeant stated. "Looked to me like the varmints tried to lead us smack into an ambush."

"They're full o' cute tricks," another agreed. "Every day it gits worse."

Just after dusk the snow came and Sheldon crawled into his bunk with at least one consolation. He didn't have to stand guard out there in the bitter night. Being a civilian had its advantages.

On the following day he was out in the gloom of late dawn, ready to get his wagons unloaded, but even so the post was astir earlier. The snow had proved to be light and Colonel Carrington had issued fresh orders for the day, evidently aimed at preparing for winter.

Wagons that had not been used on the previous day were being loaded with heavy planks and stringers for a bridge that was to be thrown across Big Piney at the island. Apparently Carrington hoped to continue lumbering operations in spite of the increasing cold. At nine o'clock twenty wagons and a large crew of construction workers went out, escorted by sixty mounted men under Carrington himself. All other timber operations were suspended for the day.

Sheldon counted himself lucky. He had his own wagons unloaded soon enough so that he could have most of the day to himself — and late enough so none of them would be drafted for the bridge-building party. He saw to it that men, mules and wagons were in good condition, then he went into the fort. The temperature was still dropping and there was no point in staying out in the cold when he didn't have to.

He spent a few hours visiting with Captain Brown in the quartermaster's office but in mid-afternoon word came that a Crow scout named Rolling Bear had just reported in to Adjutant Phisterer. The scout said he had found much trouble in getting through the Sioux patrols. Many of the raiding parties from the south were now concentrating around Phil Kearny.

Harriet Winthrop came in while he and Brown discussed the chances of the Indians laying siege to the post. "I understand that the fort is almost surrounded," she said tersely. "I also hear that some empty wagons will leave for Fort Reno next week. I want you to cancel our contract and take our wagons with that train."

Sheldon glanced at Brown and chuckled without mirth. "Word sure does get around. Sorry, Miss Winthrop, but I'm afraid that would be jumping out of the frying pan smack into the fire."

"But things are going from bad to worse here. I think we should save our property while there's still a chance."

150

"There's no chance," Brown cut in. "Our trains have been under attack for five months now. If the Sioux are really closing in they'll make sure to cut off all communication. You'll be safer here than on the road."

She bit her lip and looked out across the wintry hills toward the Big Horns. Sheldon's swift grin came and went. "I suppose you're thinking that I got us into this by taking that wood contract. At least we're still drawing contract fees."

"What good is that if we lose everything?"

"No good — but if it happens, you and I won't be around to feel bad about loss of profits."

"That's a brutal way to put it!"

"It's the truth. I just thought I'd mention it so you could be real sore at me while you're at it. I didn't return to Laramie with the wagons. Because I didn't come back you had to come up here and see why. You couldn't get away again. So I'll be to blame if the Sioux get you or the wagons or both. Go ahead and blame me."

She shook her head angrily. "You don't have to be so sarcastic. I'm not blaming you. I think your deal with the army was a good one. I certainly can't blame you because I was unable to mind my own business. And I don't blame you for the possible loss of the wagons. You couldn't foresee this mess any more than the United States Army seems to have done."

He stared at her for a long minute, wondering whether the pink in her cheeks was a show of embarrassment or just the effect of having been out in

151

the December wind. "Thanks," he said finally. "I feel better."

Captain Pierce burst into the room at that point. "That Indian had news for me, Sheldon!" he exclaimed. "He knows where Crabiel's cabin is. The scout had to go back into the Big Horns to avoid some war parties and he saw the place. He also saw a man he describes as a madman so I guess it would be Crabiel."

"Is the fort really surrounded?" Harriet asked.

Pierce nodded but didn't even look toward her. "The cabin is on Rock Creek. Do you think I might have a chance to get through the Indians and find it? Rolling Bear confirms Captain Powell in his report of large numbers."

Harriet turned without another word and went out. Pierce did not even know that she was annoyed at him. "How far is Rock Creek, Sheldon?" he asked, his excitement still high.

Brown gave Sheldon the wink and commented, "I'll bet the lady is pretty miffed to have Pierce come in here and bust up her talk. Sounds like she's mighty uneasy over the Indian news."

Sheldon took the cue. "She won't scare easy. It's just that she's always been so anxious to make herself a good business woman. Always trying to prove herself to her father. Now her conscience is hurting her. She thinks this mess may get worse and she's blaming herself for not finding a way out before it was too late."

Brown had intended only to belittle the interests of Pierce, as a friendly bit of badinage, but he suddenly realized that Sheldon had made sense with his reply. "I

152

think you've got it!" he said. "That's what keeps her on edge all of the time. She's trying too hard not to make any mistakes."

"Same thing that's wrong with most of us," Sheldon told him. "I try too hard to be a successful contractor. You try too hard to be a hero. Maybe both of us ought to ease up."

Brown chuckled. "We went into that before. Anyway my transfer came through. I go to Laramie with the first wagon train, for appointment to an infantry command. No more groceries for Fred Brown!"

"This is serious!" Pierce interrupted, clearly exasperated. "I've got to find this man Crabiel. How would it be if I went with that train you mention, Brown? I could leave it and head for Rock Creek after we get through the Indian lines."

"It wouldn't take you close," Sheldon warned. "The trail runs to the southeast and Rock Creek — or the part where that cabin ought to be — is almost due west-southwest of here."

"Wait until spring," Brown advised. "Winter's no time for such a jaunt."

"It may be my only chance. I can't risk it when the Indians are covering the country with their scouting parties. Maybe they'll hole up for the winter when the snow comes. Then I could get through."

"Not a bad idea," Sheldon agreed, simply trying to humor him.

"You like it? Fine. How would it be if you were to go along with me? You've got an axe to grind, you know. Getting Crabiel could clear up all of the mystery connected with this whole matter. When the snow comes your wagons won't be able to move and you can . . ."

"Not so fast," Sheldon protested. "I just said it would be . . ."

Pierce wasn't paying any attention. "Meanwhile I'll volunteer for guard service with the wood trains. That'll give me a a chance to brush up on my scouting. In another couple of weeks I'll have old Bridger looking like a beginner!"

Brown laughed aloud. "That will be something! Several thousand whites and ten times as many Indians have spent forty years trying to make Jim Bridger look bad. You're really ambitious!"

They separated in good spirits, Sheldon going outside to see the bridge crew come in. From all reports the day had been completely peaceful. Colonel Carrington was even a bit skeptical about the reported masses of Indians in the vicinity. He had scouted with his mounted escort and had seen no Indian trails in the new-fallen snow.

There was a general atmosphere of optimism about the camp that night. Maybe this meant the end of the siege. It was well known that Indians had neither the organization nor the temperament for siege operations and it seemed likely that they had disbanded before the approach of winter.

In the teamsters' barracks that night Smoke Prine dug out his banjo for the first time in weeks, a brand-new verse indicating how he had spent his off-duty afternoon.

154

We chop the trees and haul the wood
And fight the Sioux each day.
We're buildin' Fort Phil Kearny just
To keep the skunks at bay.
We don't care if it rains or snows
Or if the nights git cold.
When Injun fingers start to freeze,
Them pests won't act so bold.

It didn't make much difference that the chorus was ragged, a half-dozen different sets of words being used by the singers. Morale had taken a turn for the better.

CHAPTER
FOURTEEN

Another dawn found the weather still threatening but with no new snow on the ground. The thermometer had risen a little during the night but the lightly powdered, frozen ground would still make hauling an easy matter. The wood trains were readied as soon as it was light but no orders came for over an hour. Scouting parties had gone out earlier and it appeared that the Indians were to be located before the train would move.

When the scouts returned, having seen no Indians, the forty wagons moved promptly. A slight break in the weather developed at the same time and some of the men were singing as they drove away. Maybe the worst was over.

It took some time to get the double column rolling, the lead wagons having to hold back until the line was properly formed, but at ten o'clock they moved off at a fast pace, mounted infantry out ahead while other soldiers shouldered their Springfields along the line. With the more moderate weather the men had discarded their buffalo coats and looked more like soldiers than the shaggy bears of the last few days.

To Sheldon near the head of the column it was quite a scene. Directly in front of him a half-dozen mounted men were silhouetted against the snow-flecked spruces and pines of the mountain slopes while above this dark border of evergreens loomed the peaks of the Big Horns. Some of them were smothered by the still lowering clouds but others stood out starkly white in the patches of sunlight that broke through. The scene was one of brilliant but rather gloomy grandeur.

For a little over a mile the road ran within sight of the fort but then it wound around a shoulder of the Sullivant Hills and the fort was lost to view. They covered a second mile without trouble but suddenly a crash of gunfire sounded from directly ahead. One of the mounted men went down but scrambled to his feet to run back toward the train while his companions answered the ambush fire. Other shots rattled along the line as the wagons went into their defense positions.

"Gittin' hasty, ain't they?" Prine shouted at Sheldon. "They ain't lettin' us git outa earshot o' the fort now."

"Nor within range," Sheldon called back. "That's pretty long-distance fire — and not very accurate." After going through so many of these raids he thought he could tell something about them from the sound. This one didn't sound like much. No mounted warriors had come out to use their usual dashing tactics and the rifle fire was neither heavy nor damaging.

The men held their defense positions and waited, a flat silence descending upon the scene. After a few minutes one of the fort's cannon boomed but this time they could not hear the explosion of the shell. Either the gunners were using solid shot or they were aiming in some other direction.

They could see the guard on Pilot Hill making signals but not to the train. Evidently he had reported the attack and was now relaying orders to the relief column. The fort cannon boomed again and this time Sheldon thought he could hear the shell exploding. He couldn't be certain that it wasn't an echo so it told him nothing.

The Indian fire had ceased entirely but the men waited, minutes dragging along without any sight of enemy or relief troops. A guard officer took a patrol out but failed to stir up anything. The wagon men were getting restless by that time, anxious to get on with the day's work, but the guard lieutenant was cautious. Those cannon shots sounded like something big afoot; he didn't propose to do anything rash.

Then the guard on Pilot Hill began to signal again, this time giving the train an order to proceed. At once the wagons moved forward, everyone half-relieved, and half-annoyed at the petty detention.

For the rest of the day the only matter of interest was the new bridge over Big Piney Fork. The engineers had made a good job and the infantrymen who had been forced to wade through icy water on previous guard tours were especially appreciative. The woodcutters quickly chopped down enough trees to make loads for the wagons that could not be loaded from the already-cut supply and the train moved out across the bridge again.

Halfway back to the fort a messenger met them, demanding to know what had happened to Captains Fetterman and Ten Eyck. Sheldon could hear the question and see the man's obvious amazement when he was informed that neither officer had been seen by the wood train.

"Ye heard the shootin', didn't ye?" the courier demanded of the sergeant he had addressed. "They been doin' an awful lot of it back there!"

"All we heard was axes choppin', mules brayin' and men cussin'," the sergeant told him. "We didn't know any relief was out."

The messenger cursed grimly and galloped back along the line of wagons. Sheldon waited until they were once more along the slopes of the Sullivant Hills and then rode up toward the summit. From there he could hear an occasional distant shot. Someone was having a fight over beyond Lodge Trail Ridge. Probably Fetterman and Ten Eyck had come out with a relief party but had tried to flank the savages by going around the opposite side of the hill. Maybe they had even managed to trap some of the bushwhackers.

The firing died away as he listened so he rode back to the train, alert against the chance of a raid by casual stragglers. They reached the fort without trouble, however — to find that all was excitement there. It took a little time to get the story in anything like coherent form but gradually the picture took shape. When the wood train was first reported under attack there were several demonstrations by other small bands of Indians near the fort. These had been sent flying by howitzer shells while a strong column under Captain Fetterman was sent to the aid of the wood train. Fetterman's immediate command had been made up of fifty

159

mounted infantrymen from four separate companies but he had been accompanied by Lieutenant Grummond with thirty troopers who had come to Fort Phil Kearny with the last wagon train to get through. The two civilian scouts, Wheatly and Fisher, had accompanied the force and it was supposed that Captain Brown had also managed to go along. At least he was missing.

They had ridden around the north side of the Sullivant Hills with the apparent intention of catching the raiders from the rear. When they appeared within view of the Pilot Hill observer again they were on the summit of Lodge Trail Ridge, deployed in a skirmish line. At that point the lookout had signaled that the train was moving again but they had paid no attention, going down the northern slope of the ridge in direct violation of Carrington's orders.

Sound of firing had immediately resulted and the lookout could see Indians on the ridge which Fetterman's men had just left. He reported that the relief column was surrounded and Colonel Carrington promptly dispatched Captain Ten Eyck with seventy-six more men, using up the entire duty roster.

Since that moment nothing definite was known. Ten Eyck had sent a messenger back to request a cannon and the howitzer had been sent. There had been no further word and no additional sounds of fighting.

"We missed somethin'," Smoke Prine remarked with a wry grin. "All that goin' on while we was down in the woods limberin' up our muscles!"

"Lucky for us. If two strong forces met trouble — as it now appears — we'd have been in a sweet mess if we'd had to fight our way back."

One of the howitzers had been placed to cover the wagon camp, expecting that an attack might be launched against that weak spot. There had been no sight of an enemy on that side since the case shot broke up the early demonstration but no one was taking useless chances. Every woodcutter and driver who could handle a gun was taking a post for defense. Sheldon's men moved into thin places in the line and then Sheldon went on into the fort itself.

He saw anxiety on every face. When Ten Eyck left with the entire duty roster there had been a hasty mustering of the sick, the clerks, the guardhouse inmates and any other man capable of pointing a rifle. They were now huddled on the catwalk inside the palisade, ready for whatever might happen. The good humor of the previous evening had changed to stark dread.

Pierce met him as he came through the gate, asking the question that must have been asked of every man who had come in. "Sure you didn't see anything of Fetterman or Ten Eyck?"

"We didn't even know they'd come out. No troops came near us."

"You'd better stay here with me. Even now that the train guards are back we're still desperate for men. I'm in charge of this angle of the wall and I'd like to draft you as my aide. Will you do it?"

Sheldon smiled. "Getting to be a combat officer, eh?" he chuckled. "Don't get any ambitions like Brown. I hear he's in the saddle again without orders."

Pierce nodded. "He wanted to have a crack at the Sioux before he gets transferred to Laramie."

"I hope he remembers poor Bingham. That kind of ambition is sometimes hard on the would-be hero and also on the poor devils who have to go out with him on his glory hunt."

"He has no command," Pierce said shortly. Then he added with a thin smile, "It puts a crimp in some of my ambitions. I think Crabiel can wait."

Every post continued to be manned and the silent tension was indicative of what everyone was thinking. They expected a major attack. That meant they were afraid the Indians had already won a victory in the hills. The thought was sobering enough to make Sheldon check the loads in his Colt. Pierce saw the move and grinned again. Neither man needed to say a word.

Presently Smoke came in through the gate, his face showing relief at sight of Sheldon. "Glad ye're handy, Ross. I didn't like the idee of huntin' through the fort fer ye."

"Trouble at the wagons?" Sheldon asked quickly.

"Nope. I just heard that Enright lit a shuck this afternoon."

"You mean he's gone?"

"Yep. He was drivin' one o' Grull's wagons, the ones the army took over when Grull got killed. He was still with it when we went onto Piney Island but he wasn't around when it was time to come back. A sojer had to drive her in."

"Any chance that an Indian picked him off?"

"Not likely. Wasn't none around at that time. I figger he lit out to find Crabiel. It sure ain't no happen-so that he busted loose right after the Crow arrived with news of old Crabby."

Pierce looked up with interest. "Then the rumor is around?"

"Sure. That Injun is a gossiper. Everybody in the wagon camp knowed about it right away."

Before they could discuss it there was a hail from somewhere along the defense line and a sentry pointed to Pilot Hill. The picket up there was making signals again, this time reporting that Captain Ten Eyck's column was returning, apparently in full strength and with their wagons.

Harriet Winthrop came to Sheldon's post a few minutes later. "Is it true that Ten Eyck's men are coming back alone?" she asked in a low voice.

"That's the report," he told her soberly. "We've had no word of the others. I'm afraid they may be in trouble." He was speaking especially of Captain Brown and assumed that she understood what he meant.

When she moved away in silence he wondered what it must be like in the quarters of the married officers. Lieutenant Grummond's wife must be having a mighty anxious day.

The December dusk was lowering when Ten Eyck's column reached the fort. Even in the gathering gloom the watchers on the walls knew that there had been a major disaster. Sheldon counted seventy-seven mounted men and two wagon drivers, the exact number that had gone out, but the ammunition wagons were piled high with bodies and many of the soldiers were leading extra horses bearing similar grisly evidence.

Pierce counted swiftly as the column came through the gates, making his calculations in a voice that was husky with shock but still audible to those around him. "A hundred and sixty men went out of here, not counting orderlies who have already returned. Now I see seventy-nine alive and forty-nine dead. Where are the others?"

No one tried to answer. They knew no answer was forthcoming or expected.

Torches had been brought to the area between the stables and the enlisted men's barracks, so the returning troops moved into a half-light that was compounded of threatening darkness and flickering pine knots. Forty-nine men who had ridden out of Fort Phil Kearny at noon were now being unloaded upon the ground as grim reminders of the kind of war the Sioux would fight. Every corpse had been stripped bare and viciously mutilated. A wave of nausea swept through the garrison and for long minutes after the return of the column there was little desire to hear the details. No one wanted to talk, particularly the men who had drawn the horrible task of handling the hideous, frozen bodies.

Sheldon remained just long enough to make certain of a couple of facts, then he walked away rapidly, trying to keep his composure. As he approached Officers Row

164

Harriet Winthrop came out to meet him, her lips tight. "Brown and Fetterman are both dead," he told her, his voice not as steady as he would have liked to make it. "They don't know about Grummond. He's among the thirty or so that are missing."

"Thank you," she said steadily. "I'll tell Mrs. Grummond that there is that much hope left."

When he went back to his post on the palisade, military necessity was beginning to assert itself once more. Officers were making their rounds, prodding sentries into watchfulness and making a stern effort to dispel the numb gloom which had descended upon the entire garrison. Already a detail had been sent to prepare the bodies for a mass burial.

Pierce brought an account of the known details when he returned from a hasty supper. Captain Ten Eyck's column had headed directly for the point where the firing had seemed loudest, following the same trail Fetterman had used to the summit of Lodge Trail Ridge. Just before they reached the crest the firing died out completely and from the top of the elevation they could see no sign of the other detachment. There were plenty of Indians in the valley of Peno Creek, however, and Ten Eyck sent his men to the attack, expecting a sharp fight.

To his astonishment the Indians retreated. At first he thought the Sioux had mistaken his baggage wagons for artillery and were getting away from the dreaded canister. Then his troops came upon the battleground and no one took much interest in the Indian retreat as a wave of nausea hit the group. Dead men seemed to be everywhere, the quantity of arrows littering the ground and bristling from corpses offering ample testimony that the command had been surrounded and over-whelmed. Only a few of the dead had died by bullets. Captains Fetterman and Brown had died within reach of each other, each with a bullet in the head. Either they had killed each other at the last moment or had committed suicide.

Ten Eyck promptly ordered a halt. It was clear that Fetterman had disobeyed the orders not to cross Lodge Trail Ridge and had been led into a deadly trap by the handful of warriors who had retreated before his first attack. Ten Eyck did not propose to make the same mistake. He ordered the bodies picked up and began a retreat.

The Indians who had been retreating before him promptly took up the pursuit but did not press it, either because they were content with the earlier victory or because they were disappointed at the failure of their second ruse.

His rear guard reported that the retreating column was followed by some six hundred or more Sioux but there was no attack. The Indians remained just out of rifle range halfway back to Phil Kearny and then disappeared. Even with no direct evidence on the subject the story was fairly clear. The half-hearted attack on the wood train had been simply a device to get a relief column into the hills. Then a small number of Indians had retreated before that column, drawing it into a deadly ambush. No one held out any hopes for the missing men under Lieutenant Grummond. They could not have survived.

Lights burned in Colonel Carrington's office until nearly dawn as plans were made to withstand the general attack which everyone assumed would be coming. In Officers Row other lights burned, the wives of other officers trying to console Mrs. Grummond. On the palisades the guard had been doubled, the men keeping each other alert with muttered comments. On every tongue was the grim thought of the morrow, old Indian fighters well aware that such a victory for the warriors would probably be just what they needed to fire them up for a mass assault on the post. Indians who had taken no hand in the Fetterman disaster would be burning to match the deeds of their brethren. A short-handed, improperly armed, badly munitioned garrison was due to receive the attack of anywhere from one to three thousand triumphant warriors.

CHAPTER
FIFTEEN

Not all of the talk was apprehensive. Some of it was the expression of a sullen anger on the part of men who felt that their comrades had been sacrificed to the ambition for personal glory. Captain Brown had been noted for his desire to draw some sort of brevet and he had accompanied the troops without orders. Fetterman had been bad enough but Brown had been worse. The two had worked up a contest for personal laurels and had disobeyed Carrington's specific orders by taking men into Peno Valley. Enlisted men wasted little sympathy on either; they grew bitter as they rated Fetterman and Brown as the virtual murderers of the men who had obeyed their orders.

Sheldon left the palisade when Pierce was relieved by a regular officer and he discovered quickly that the provost officer was still thinking in terms of his own objectives.

"What chance would Enright have had to get through the Sioux?" Pierce asked as they headed across toward his quarters.

"Hard to tell. He might have been lucky. Fetterman was trapped almost due north of Piney Island. If every Indian in the vicinity rushed to get in on the kill, as they probably did, it's possible that the hills to the south of the island might have been clear most of the afternoon. Enright might have picked the one moment of the winter when his chance of a breakthrough was best."

"Is it possible that he would have known of the Sioux plans?"

"I doubt it. He heard about Crabiel and he wanted to get away. The train was attacked along the trail but not at the island. Likely it seemed that there was a lull he could use. I don't think there's any chance he could have been in communication with the Indians."

"It's still a bad deal. He knows I'm after Crabiel. Obviously he also has some powerful reason to find the man — and to find him before I do. If he gets there first I'm afraid my chances are finished."

"Maybe he didn't get through. Not all of the Sioux were in Peno Valley yesterday."

"Did he have a horse?"

"I don't think so. We'll know before long, though. Smoke Prine will be asking plenty of questions around the wagon barracks tonight."

When a red sun climbed out of the eastern buttes the garrison seemed to draw a collective deep breath. The expected dawn attack had not materialized. A reinforced guard on Pilot Hill reported that there were no Indians to be seen in any direction.

Colonel Carrington ordered a bold move. Eighty men under his personal command went out with a dozen wagons to the summit of Lodge Trail Ridge. It was a risky operation but it had the effect of stopping some of the muttering. Men whose lives were still in deadly peril found it somehow comforting to know that their commander would take a greater risk for himself in order to insure decent care of the bodies of the fallen.

Sheldon's thoughts were a little more practical. Before he talked to Prine about the matter of Enright's disappearance it might be a good idea to ask a few questions among the wood-train guards. Maybe some of the soldiers had seen Enright leave.

He found that particular platoon on sentry duty along the northeast wall and almost immediately spotted the bearded corporal he had come to know rather well. He didn't try to conceal the nature of his errand.

"I suppose you heard that a driver named Enright slipped away from the train yesterday. We think he deserted, not even knowing that a fight was in progress. We even think we know why he went. Got any ideas to offer?"

There was an odd look in the man's eyes as he stared at Sheldon. He seemed on the point of replying with some feeling but then he looked away and growled, "Why should I? I didn't see the polecat go."

"This is not official," Sheldon persisted, feeling certain that the corporal had something that he could tell. "He wasn't an enlisted man so it's not desertion. He had a right to go, I suppose. I'm just curious to know if he had a horse or provisions with him. Not that it would have made much difference if he happened to run into any Indians."

170

"Hope the Sioux got him!" the man snapped. "He had it comin'."

"Sounds like you didn't like him."

"Nothin' personal. He didn't even know me. I jest knowed who he was from a spell back. Served him right if he lost his scalp!"

"Then I suppose you know why he left. It doesn't seem to be much of a secret around here this morning."

"You mean he's after Crabiel? Then I reckon you're right."

"Tell me about it," Sheldon invited. "I've been in a bad tangle on this Enright business and I'd like to clear it up just to get myself out of it. Do you know if there's any truth in the idea that Crabiel was sent out here by the Confederate government to stir up the Indians as a diversion?"

The man grunted unhappily. "I reckon we might as well git it over," he said. "Ain't no harm in tellin' the yarn now. Crabiel was just what you said. He was supposed to make so much trouble that a lot o' Yank troops would be sent out here. That would ease the pressure on our — I mean the Southern armies."

"You don't have to hide anything," Sheldon told him. "You told me some time ago that you served in the Confederate army. You don't have to worry about it or be ashamed of it. Where does Enright fit in?"

"He's the man sent Crabiel. His name was Ennis in them days and he was one o' them political johnnies that got hisself a cheap commission. Because he talked like a Yank they put him into some kind o' spy work. That was when he worked Crabiel through the lines and sent him out here with a lot o' good hard cash to work up some Injun troubles. Fer a long time we didn't hear nothin' more about either of 'em. I got took at Lookout Mountain and spent some time in Rock Island prison before I volunteered to take Injun service with the Yanks and git outa prison. While I was at Rock Island I heard that Enright had been took."

"I see. Then it looks as if Enright maybe had some kind of a deal with Crabiel to hold part of the money he was supposed to spend, the pair of them to divide it up when the chance presented itself. Is that the way you see it?"

"Somethin' like that. They toted a real bundle of greenbacks through the lines, enough to put four-five men like Crabiel into business with the Injuns. No Confederate currency neither!"

"It fits," Sheldon said thoughtfully. "Maybe Crabiel kept the whole bundle — and now Enright wants his share of the loot."

"That's the way I figger it. They're fixin' to split the money that shoulda been used fer men in the lines what needed it bad. I reckon you kin see why I ain't real happy to see 'em get away with it."

"You seem to know quite a bit about it," Sheldon observed quietly.

"Good reason. I was the one got 'em through the lines when they went." He grinned sourly as he added, "In our army a man didn't need to have much education to git a commission. We was mostly interested in fightin'."

Sheldon nodded a bit ruefully. "Maybe it was better that way."

"But don't think I'm goin' to be no witness," the corporal went on. "Most o' what I said was guesswork."

"I'll keep you out of it. And thanks. We'll see what can be done."

He went directly to Pierce's quarters, reporting both the facts and the theory. Pierce didn't bother to dispute any part of it. Everything fitted too well. Enright had come west under odd circumstances, using his connection with Winthrop for that purpose and deserting the job as soon as he reached Laramie. On the way out he had asked questions, smothering his obvious dislike of Sheldon to make himself temporarily affable when he discovered that Sheldon had spent some time in the Powder River country. When Sheldon let him know that his interest in Milo Crabiel had been noted he had become so angry that he had started a fight. Later, afraid Sheldon might publish his secret, he had tried to silence Sheldon by making out a case against him. That move had tended to get Sheldon out of the way and at the same time put Pierce on the wrong scent. Finally he had taken a job as a wagon driver in order to get himself into the part of the country where Crabiel was reported to be.

"Sounds like a tight case," Sheldon said finally. "But the case against me sounded pretty tight too. Let's keep it quiet until we know a bit more. We can't make a move now anyway."

At the wagon barracks he found that Smoke had not been idle. Instead of asking questions he had started a general round of gossip and one of the woodcutters had told of seeing a man slipping away among the trees

173

shortly after the train started to load. From the description it was certainly Enright. The woodchopper stated that the man had been wearing a buffalo coat and was carrying a parcel of some sort. He had not seen any weapon so had not realized that the fellow was leaving the camp. But for the buffalo coat he probably wouldn't have noticed him at all but the men had been wearing lighter clothing that day and the coat had caught his attention.

"Six gun under the coat," Prine told Sheldon. "Likely that was the way he did it."

"I wonder how far he managed to go?"

"Mebbe we'll know 'fore long. The Colonel's boys might haul in the carcass. It ain't likely the heathens let him git away."

Sheldon did not mention the possibility he had discussed with Pierce, that Enright's chances had been particularly good at that one time. It was just as well not to let the gossip spread any more. Enright and Crabiel were small potatoes compared to the dire straits of Fort Phil Kearny.

In mid-afternoon Colonel Carrington's force returned, bringing with them thirty-two more corpses. A check of the duty roster showed that the tally was now complete. There had been no survivors.

A careful survey of the battlefield indicated that the earlier guesses had been accurate, that the command had been annihilated when Fetterman sent his men into a well-laid trap. Many of them had not survived the first Sioux assault but a few had done damage to the enemy. Wheatly and Fisher, the two civilian scouts, had gone down only after a hard battle. There were bloodstains all around their position and nearly a hundred empty cartridge cases littered the ground beside their bodies. Those Henry repeaters had taken a heavy toll of the Indians but in the end the warriors had overwhelmed them.

Again that night the post went under double guard, civilians serving with the soldiers. It was now believed that the Indian losses had been so heavy that the Sioux had withdrawn to reorganize. That had given the defenders a day of respite but now they must expect an attack.

Just before dusk the clouds piled up again behind the Big Horns and the thermometer began to drop. At noon it had been in the low thirties; at five o'clock it was down to ten and falling fast. Mess had become a continuous affair, men eating in small shifts so that the palisades might always have a strong guard on duty. Hot food at frequent intervals was the order of the night. Pickets stamping along the guard walks on the walls would need its sustenance as the bitter wind howled at them.

Sheldon walked a post until eight o'clock and by that time the snowfall was a good hour old and increasing with every blast from the Big Horns. At ten the guard went on one-hour detail in order to avoid frostbite. At midnight all able-bodied men were called into emergency service. Drifts were piling up along the palisade until there was danger that an attacker might climb right up and over the walls.

A shoveling detail was added to the guard, men clearing the drifts to form a sort of moat outside the palisade. By that time the thermometer registered twelve below zero and the storm was howling with increased fury. Men worked desperately, both to keep from freezing and because they knew the importance of what they were doing. Reason told them that even Sioux would not be hardy enough to mount an attack on such a night but apprehension was stronger than reason. All a man had to do was to remember those frozen, mutilated corpses under their blanket of snow on the parade ground and he forced himself to forget freezing fingers.

Sheldon was awakened just before five o'clock, having slept only a couple of hours. He came out of his blankets at once, thinking he was due to go on duty again, but discovered that Captain Pierce was standing over him.

"Sorry to get you up, Sheldon," Pierce said, suppressed excitement in his voice, "but I think this is our chance. The storm is just as bad as ever and the temperature is down to minus thirty. I think we can get through to the mountains without any Indians being around to intercept us."

Sheldon stared. In weather too bad for the Indians he was being asked to go out on a wild-goose chase. "You're out of your mind," he growled. "Go back to bed."

"It's the only chance to get through. Phillips tried it."

"What Phillips?"

"John Phillips. That miner fellow who's been scouting for the regiment. Colonel Carrington asked for a volunteer to ride to Laramie for help. Phillips was the only one who said it wasn't impossible. He left an hour ago on the Colonel's horse."

"That's nerve!" Sheldon exclaimed, more awake now. "Two hundred and sixty miles of snow and Indians! Still, it seems like the best bet. When the storm eases up the Sioux will be on the watch again."

"That's just the point. If it's the chance for Phillips it's the chance for us. I'm taking you at your word, of course, that you are willing to help. I could never do it alone, I know. That's why I talked the Colonel out of asking you to volunteer before Phillips made his offer." He grinned thinly as he added the final remark.

"Then you've got permission for us to go?"

"Yes. The fort is pretty secure now and the snow will hamper attackers, driving them into the open where the howitzers can work them over. Neither of us have any duty here. Your wagons won't work for a long time and my real duty is to get out there after Enright."

Sheldon aimed a tight smile at him. "I'll tell you one thing," he said grimly. "Not all of the idiots are on the Peace Commission!"

They made preparations hastily, both bundling into two suits of underwear and extra socks. Oversize boots, buffalo coats with hoods, extra mittens and other winter gear made them reasonably safe against the blizzard. A staff sergeant secured horses for them, picking big animals rather than fast ones, at Sheldon's request. Both wore six-guns and Sheldon borrowed a

Spencer carbine from a bandsman who was in the hospital. He had some qualms about taking even one weapon from the fort but was persuaded to do so when it was pointed out that every Spencer in the place was held by a man who had been given no practice with the weapon. One gun and a half-dozen cartridges would not make much difference to the defense of the fort.

It lacked five minutes to six o'clock when they rode out through the drifts into the whirling storm. Two minutes later they could not even see the lights of the fort and Sheldon took the precaution of putting a line on Pierce's horse. Even old mountain men could get separated in this kind of storm.

They found their way by judging slopes, floundering through the drifts in what Sheldon hoped was a general southerly direction. It made him wonder how Jack Phillips ever expected to stick to his trail for a matter of two hundred and sixty miles.

There was danger of running across Indian encampments in the creek bottoms so they kept to the slopes where there was a bit of protection from upland timber. At the end of what Sheldon thought was a full hour they were crossing a shoulder which ought to be Fort Ridge, a slight lessening in the gloom warning that daybreak was not far away.

The snow slackened with the dawn, making their progress a little less painful but increasing the chance of discovery. There was one small break in the storm which permitted Sheldon to look out across a flat white expanse which he guessed was Lake De Smet. If that guess was correct they were pretty well beyond the

178

main Sioux concentrations, probably on the spur of the Big Horns which separated the valleys of Big Piney and Rock Creek.

Most of the time they were leading their horses now, both of them fighting off the bitter chill by getting the additional exercise. It was painfully slow work but time was no longer important; the vital consideration was to make sure that they didn't stumble onto a detached band of Indians.

Shortly after what they thought was noon they halted in a patch of thick timber and built a fire, the hungry horses nibbling at spruce boughs while the men made coffee and munched hardtack. Other provisons had to be hoarded against an hour of greater need.

They halted again as soon as dusk began to fall, picking the thickest cover they could find and knocking together a lean-to of heavy pine boughs. Again they risked a fire, knowing that warm food would be important before the bitter night that was ahead of them.

They slept only when exhaustion became stronger than the misery of cold but at daybreak they moved on once more, the blizzard still raging. It was even slower than on the previous day, the snow having deepened to make progress that much more difficult. Several times they blundered into drifts which they could not break through, and had to lead the horses back and find a tedious way around. Still Sheldon insisted on sticking to the timber, partly for shelter from the storm and enemy and partly because there was less glare under the trees.

They dropped down into the valley of Rock Creek shortly after noon, using extra care against the chance that stormbound Indians might have taken shelter here. The storm seemed to have slackened a little but still they could see no indication that anyone had passed this point.

"Which way now?" Pierce asked huskily. "The Crow just said Rock Creek. I don't know how far up it."

"Not too far, I'd guess," Sheldon replied. "Rolling Bear probably didn't go too far back into the hills. He was just staying clear of open country."

He hoped the guess was right. It didn't seem likely that Pierce could take much more of the hardship they had been enduring.

There was added danger now as they groped their way along steep banks to the east. Travel would have been easier on the ice of the creek but the risk was too great. They could not afford to blunder on Crabiel's shack without warning any more than they could gamble on being seen by the Sioux.

When they made camp for the night they had seen neither the cabin nor an Indian. They climbed the ridge a little, again using the cover of thick forest and spending a night that was just as bitter as the previous one. Still neither complained. They had withstood the blizzard without frostbite and they had avoided war parties. Under the circumstances a man couldn't ask for more.

CHAPTER
SIXTEEN

Another morning found the storm abated but with the cold still intense. Both men kept their faces covered but still it was painful to breathe. They took time for a decent breakfast, risking a fire of the dry pine boughs which could be stripped dry from partly dead trees. They made a hot fire and almost no smoke.

Suddenly Sheldon thought of something. "Merry Christmas," he said with a wry grin. "Find anything in your stocking?"

Pierce twisted cracked lips in an answering grin. "A blamed cold foot," he replied. "And a colder one in the other stocking!"

They pushed on down Rock Creek until there was nothing but open country ahead. "Looks like I guessed wrong," Sheldon growled. "Rolling Bear must have been playing it safer than I figured."

Pierce did not reply, simply swinging his horse to start over the back trail. For a moment there came a hunch on Sheldon's part to take the stream bed for their return trip but then he thought better of it. A second set of tracks meant added danger and by retracing they could use a trail that had already been broken.

The sun rose behind them and they pulled their caps lower, trying to block that dangerous glare. They passed the spot where they had gone up the ridge to spend the night, then the trail where they had come down into the valley first. Both moved in silence now, aware that Crabiel's place had to be close at hand. Evidently they had only missed it by a short distance when they first came across the ridge.

They spotted the shack at almost the same instant, Pierce calling a hoarse warning just as Sheldon threw up a hand for a halt. The hut stood in a little clump of piñons not far above the creek, a sturdy little place of logs with a mud and stone chimney.

"No tracks in the snow," Pierce said. "Suppose he's inside?"

"No smoke. Looks like we missed him."

"What about Enright? Think he showed up?"

"That's the part I don't like. Enright had at least a day and a half before the snow fell. If he got through the Sioux he could have been here as early as the morning of the twenty-third. The pair of them could have gone away before the snow fell that evening."

He outlined their approach and they separated, Pierce going down to cross the creek below the hut while Sheldon circled and came down from upstream. There was no alarm as the two men closed in cautiously and within a matter of minutes they stood side by side at the door. The heavy pine barrier was closed but the latch still showed above the snow. Sheldon tripped it, stepping out of the line of fire as he shoved the door open.

182

Nothing happened. There was no sound from the dark interior. The three-foot depth of snow which had banked against the door began to drift into the cabin as its support was removed but otherwise the picture was an inert one, matching that smokeless chimney.

"He's gone — or they're both gone," Sheldon declared. "We hit the trail just a bit too late to catch him. I think . . ."

He broke off as he started into the place, halting so abruptly that Pierce collided with him from the rear. Then the pair of them stared silently at the gruesome thing that lay against the back wall of the shack.

Milo Crabiel hadn't died easy; he had met his death in horrible fashion — by torture.

"Sioux!" Pierce breathed in a shocked whisper. "They found him."

Sheldon was moving forward to stare down at the contorted body of the mad hermit. "No Sioux did this," he said positively. "He's stripped only to the waist. The Sioux strip their victims all the way — and cut 'em up all over. Crabiel suffered a lot of small stab wounds after his hands were tied. Not only that but his murderer left the door shut. I can't imagine an Indian doing that."

"Enright?"

"Likely. I figure he got here just before the blizzard broke. He caught Crabiel cold and tied him up the way he is now. Then he tortured him to make him tell where that money had been hidden. By the looks of the hole in the corner I'd say Crabiel must have talked before he died."

"And then Enright killed him?"

"Either that or he left him to freeze to death."

They studied the place in silence for some time, trying to get a better idea of the time factor. They could only guess that Crabiel had died before the snow came. Enright must have left the hut on the afternoon of the twenty-second, probably while the triumphant Sioux were watching Carrington's men pick up those last bodies along Peno Creek.

"I wonder how far he went before the snow caught him?" Pierce muttered.

"Not far. He didn't have a horse, so far as we know. There's no sign to indicate that Crabiel had one. He wouldn't have been able to move again until this morning. That means he's still close."

"Which way do you think he's likely to go?"

"South, I suppose. To Laramie or Casper. He wouldn't venture back to Phil Kearny. You figuring on trying to catch him?"

"Of course. It's more my duty than ever."

Sheldon knew what he meant. "Two ways he might have gone," he said slowly. "Not counting down the creek. We'd have seen him down there, I think. I'd say he went up one of the forks of this stream, planning to climb the ridge to the south and get out into open country that way. Suppose we make a try at hitting his trail right away. You take one notch and I'll take the other. Then we come back here and hole up in some kind of comfort for the night. The rest will permit us to start out in fairly good condition in the morning. If either of us see sign we'll know which way to head. If

184

we don't find anything this afternoon we'll go it blind tomorrow."

"Thanks," Pierce said simply. "That sounds like a good plan."

They carried the frozen corpse of Milo Crabiel out of the cabin, depositing it unceremoniously in the deepest snow available. Then they laid a fire from the ample wood supply, closed the door of the cabin, and mounted their horses once more. Sheldon pointed out the trail Pierce was to follow and angled away through the timber toward what looked like the next best bet. The agreement was that neither should go beyond the crest of the little divide.

The notch Sheldon took turned out to be the valley of a brawling mountain stream, its current so swift that in most places it had not completely frozen. The water gushed beneath snowbanks or around ice-encrusted boulders, making the going slippery and awkward.

No sign of the fugitive appeared, even in places where progress was blocked off by thick timber or brush. At such spots Sheldon searched carefully, knowing that twigs grew brittle in such intense cold and would have broken off if a man had tried to force a passage. He was only halfway to the top of the ridge when he decided that this was not the way Enright had come. Accordingly he turned the horse and started down the brook once more. That was when his luck ran out. The tired horse slipped on the ice, stumbled and went down in a heap, Sheldon going off over the animal's head to land belly down in the icy torrent.

He was partly stunned by the fall but managed to roll clear of the water before much of it could seep through the buffalo coat. For a moment or two he lay inert, trying to clear his head and decide how badly he had been hurt by the fall. The tingle of ice water penetrating his clothing helped to clear his head and he scrambled to his feet, aware of the danger of remaining wet with the temperature below zero.

The weary horse had regained his feet also and Sheldon looked him over with due care, making sure that the animal had suffered no real injury. Then he went back to look under the snow and ice for his carbine.

He found the weapon sticking out of the snow, apparently unbroken. He brushed away the mud from around the muzzle and cleaned the ice and muck from around the action. Proper cleaning would have to wait. The immediate need was to get back to Crabiel's shack and start a fire.

He led the horse as he resumed his downhill march, blaming himself for not having done so in the first place. They slithered together over the sleet-covered rocks that were beneath the softer snow, making good time simply because it was downgrade. Sheldon knew that he had not a moment to lose. Already the collar of his coat was freezing to his face but he kept his chin hunched into the icy part, fearful that exposure of the skin to the full blast of the wind would be even worse. His left arm was also wet and growing numb.

He had needed an hour to climb to the point where he had turned back. The return journey seemed at least twice as long and he found it difficult to convince himself that it was probably not more than twenty minutes in duration. When he caught himself thinking crazy thoughts about how it would feel to freeze solid while walking he decided to run a little. Even a couple of extra falls were better than letting numbness take charge.

He still had strength enough to picket the horse in some thick cover behind the shack, hurrying around then to almost hurl himself inside. There was an instant in which he knew a dismayed surprise at finding another man in the hut but then all emotion was blotted out. The other man's arm fell and a gun butt crashed down upon Sheldon's head. Even the buffalo cap could not cushion the blow and Sheldon knew no more.

When he regained his senses he seemed to be one vast ache. The pain in his head was just one of the aches and he supposed — somewhat dimly — that the other pains were symptoms of freezing. He saw that a small fire was gathering strength in the little fireplace and he tried to make dulled senses believe that everything was going to be all right. Somehow it didn't work out properly and he shut his eyes again, hoping that the next time he opened them he would be able to sort his ideas out a little better.

After a while he tried it again and this time the dark interior showed up more plainly in the strengthening firelight. Not that the sight was any more pleasing. He knew that he was lying on the dirt floor in a corner behind the door, a cold corner where the temperature was almost as low as it had been outside. The fire wasn't even beginning to affect him.

Worse than the cold was the sight of Dale Enright, smirking down at him from behind a scrub of beard. Enright's lips showed the effects of frostbite but the grin was maliciously triumphant.

"Glad you're wakin', Sheldon," Enright said sardonically, "I was afraid maybe I hit you too hard — and I just figured out a better way to handle you."

Sheldon frowned. He had recovered his senses enough to know that his hands were tied behind him but he couldn't believe that he was hearing correctly. Enright had no business sounding so calm or so pleased.

"Bothers you, eh?" Enright went on. "That makes it even. I was some bothered when I saw you down the creek this morning. I knew you were on my trail so I had to come back and see what you were trying to do. When you found Crab's body I knew what it meant. I had to get rid of the pair of you. The other fellow's Pierce, isn't he? I thought it was Prine at first but it looks more like Pierce."

He made it sound so casual that Sheldon still had a feeling that the whole thing was unreal. A murderer, ready to do more murders while surrounded by hostile Sioux and a thirty-below temperature, ought to sound at least a little more dramatic.

"So you made it easy for me," Enright went on after another of those nasty grins. "I was afraid it would be a problem because my gun jammed yesterday. Now you fix it good. You're the only ones can ruin me, you know. You've got to go."

Sheldon finally found his voice. "Think you'll get away with Crab's money, do you?" he asked, trying to make his chattering teeth behave so that he could sound as calm as Enright.

The other man grinned, seemingly unaware of cracked lips. "So you know about the money, do you? Not that it makes a bit of difference."

He turned away to squint out through a crack of the door. "Got to keep an eye out for Pierce," he growled. "He's tougher than I thought or he wouldn't be out here in this."

Sheldon tried to roll over but drew a warning growl from his captor. However he could feel the hard bulk against his hip and knew that Enright had not discovered the Colt beneath the bulky buffalo coat.

"Don't try anything," Enright warned him. He stooped down to pick up the carbine Sheldon had dropped, examining its action and looking to see that there was a cartridge in the chamber.

"They'll hunt for a man like Pierce," Sheldon warned, still trying to make the words come out solidly instead of in shattered pieces. "The army won't let you get away with this."

Enright turned an especially venomous grin on him. "That's the very way I figured. They'll hunt for him — and what they find ought to stir up some real talk. Pierce will be here, all right, but he'll be dead. He'll have been shot with his carbine. You'll be out there in the snow, frozen to death. It'll be easy. I just shoot

Pierce with your gun and then let you freeze. After that I cut your hands loose and go away. I guess you know what folks will think when they find the carcasses."

"Sorry I can't appreciate it."

"Others will. It's no secret that you had trouble with Pierce. Maybe you've been on good terms with him lately but he still had it in for you — and you were afraid of what he might do. So you brought him out here and shot him. Maybe they'll think you murdered old Crab too. Shooting Pierce with your gun will sew it up real neat."

He took another look out through the crack of the door and then turned toward the fire, again studying the action of the Spencer. Sheldon twisted himself with a painful effort, trying to get numb legs under him, but Enright swung back in a hurry, kicking his prisoner hard against the wall.

"Lie down, Sheldon," he said softly. "You might as well start freezing to death and get it over."

He took another look outside and again started toward the fire. Sheldon gasped, "You won't make it, Enright. The Indians won't let you through. Better make a deal with us; three men might get through."

Enright halted, shaking his head with mock solemnity. "Sheldon, I'm afraid you're much too honest for me to trust. Anyway I can take my chances. Now that you're providing me with horses I'll be in much better shape. One horse for me and one to carry the loot and some provisions." He nodded toward an ice-encrusted gunny sack that lay in an opposite corner.

190

He stood the Spencer against the wall while he added fuel to the fire. "Might as well make the place look inviting," he gloated. "Pierce ought to be real anxious when he comes back and finds a nice fire going. It's a shame I'll have to disappoint him when he comes bustin' in here to get warm, but wasn't it lucky for me I happened to spot you this morning? I might not have known you were on my trail if I hadn't holed up to wait for the storm to blow itself out."

He took another observation and stiffened. Sheldon knew what it meant. When Enright picked up the carbine again and went back to the door he let out a howl that carried all the power he could give it. "Look out, Pierce! He's in here with a gun!"

Enright was on him with a bound, grabbing him by the throat and hammering his head against the frozen floor. Sheldon did not quite lose his senses but the firelight went dim and his weary brain began to whirl once more. He knew that Enright was jamming a mitten into his mouth, binding it in place with the strings of the buffalo hood. He even heard the venomous whisper as Enright stood up again. "Lie still or I won't even let you freeze to death!" But none of it seemed important; all he could make himself remember was that he had to do something. He wasn't quite sure what it was that he had to do.

When his mind cleared Enright was at the door again, opening it just a crack to aim the carbine through. There was the soft squeak of boots in snow as Pierce came toward the cabin and Sheldon wriggled desperately once more, trying to loosen the gag.

He heard Pierce's voice saying something from outside. He saw Enright's finger begin to tighten on the Spencer's trigger, and he heaved himself with a final spurt of desperation, rolling toward the wall.

An explosion cut off the words which came from outside but Sheldon lost all knowledge of the world at the same instant, the gunshot loosening his last thin hold on consciousness. Where there had been a hazy struggle with pain and fear there was nothing but blackness.

CHAPTER
SEVENTEEN

Consciousness returned slowly, but after a while Sheldon knew that he was reasonably comfortable. His head ached and there was a tingle of frostbite in his fingers but the sense of disaster was gone. Then he realized that he was in front of a little fire, with dry blankets and robes around him. For some time that was enough. He didn't try to figure it out.

Presently Pierce's voice came to him, dimly at first but then with more clarity. "How's the head, Ross?"

Sheldon looked up with a frown. "It aches — but not like it did."

"Good. Feel up to drinking a bit of coffee? It's about ready."

He nodded, remaining silent while Pierce poured out the strong brew that had been boiling over the fire. It took a long time for him to swallow it, Pierce helping him to handle the cup, but eventually he managed it and began to feel the stimulation it gave him. The events of the day came back with a rush and he looked around with a quick frown.

"What happened to Enright?" he asked.

"Now you sound better," Pierce said, relief showing in his voice. "Enright's dead. I think his gun exploded and a piece of the lock hit him right between the eyes. I dumped the body outside." He shrugged a little as he added, "Peculiar sort of squeamishness, I suppose. I didn't want to look at him but I didn't mind dragging him out into the snow."

"Dragging bodies out of here is getting to be a habit," Sheldon said. "Let's don't keep it up." The words made him feel better. Even grim humor was better than none at all.

Pierce poured him another cup of coffee. "Want to tell me about it?" he asked. "Somehow you don't seem surprised."

"I had hopes," Sheldon told him. He related the story in some detail, dwelling on the neat little plot Enright had worked out. "It might even have worked the way he figured," he concluded. "Nobody but Brown knew that you and I were on better terms than we had been. The obvious conclusion would have been just what Enright expected. In the confusion he might have been ignored long enough for him to make a clean getaway."

"But what about the gun blowing up? That was all that saved us."

"I'll claim a small share of credit for that," Sheldon said with a wry grin. "I got some bruises so I might as well get some credit. Enright's gun was jammed; he told me so. My gun was still under my coat. That meant he would have to use the carbine."

"Which was exactly what his plan called for."

"Sure. But I was pretty sure that the carbine had its muzzle plugged with frozen mud. It went muzzle-down into the brook when I took my fall and I didn't have

194

any way to clean out the bore. Just as I began to get some of my senses back I saw him check the action but he didn't look into the muzzle. That gave me an idea. If the carbine was full of ice it would almost certainly explode if he tried to shoot it. I didn't have any other chance so I did everything I could to keep him from discovering the condition of the gun. It cost me some rough handling and a couple of nasty kicks but I kept him from taking the carbine too close to the fire. I was afraid the ice might thaw out even if he didn't find it."

Pierce shook his head wonderingly. "I guess there's not much I can say. You certainly know how I feel. I'll not forget it."

Sheldon grinned. "Not bad work for a renegade," he said modestly. "Especially one that was tied up, gagged and half-frozen. Do I get a medal?"

"Maybe you'll do better than that," Pierce told him. "The government has some kind of standing rule about the share a private citizen can claim for helping to recover money owed to the public treasury. I imagine Crabiel's loot will fall under the heading of forfeited property. That makes the government the rightful owner and you eligible for the usual percentage." He waved a hand toward the neat stacks of currency which now lay on the floor beside the sack.

"I'll buy myself a new head. This one hurts."

"One more thing and I'll let you get some sleep. Where was Enright hiding?"

"Down the creek somewhere. He saw us this morning and followed us back here because he knew he didn't dare let us live to trail him."

"That's all I wanted to know. Thanks again for making sure that he used the plugged carbine."

Sheldon's eyes were falling shut. "Merry Christmas," he said.

They spent a reasonably snug night, a howling wind serving as a constant reminder of the dead men outside. Once Sheldon awakened to the thought that their fire might betray them to any Sioux who happened to be where they could smell the smoke but he didn't let it worry him very long. Most of the headache had left him, so he simply checked his revolver and went back to sleep again.

At dawn they cooked a quantity of food so that they could carry provisions with them when they left, dousing the fire then to reduce the risk of discovery. Sheldon wanted to start for Phil Kearny at once but as soon as he tried to get around, it became apparent that he was in no condition to travel. His fall, the exposure, and the brutal kicks had bruised him so badly that it was painful for him to move. Pierce took the decision away from him.

"We'll wait," he said positively. "You can't walk and you couldn't stay on a horse. We're as safe here as anywhere."

He did picket duty during the day while Sheldon remained in the hut wrapped in robes which must have been souvenirs of Crabiel's earlier Indian trade. Toward night it began to snow again and they risked another fire.

196

It was still snowing next morning so they let the fire burn, feeling reasonably safe from the Sioux while the storm lasted. Some of Sheldon's aches were gone now and he took over the cooking while Pierce made a more complete inventory of the gunny sack's contents. In addition to the bank notes there was a small locked tin box. They could only guess why Enright had taken it along without opening it. Probably he had been anxious to get away from the bloody mess he had made.

"I'll leave it the way it is," Pierce decided. "If it contains records that tell part of the story it will be just as well for somebody else to unlock the box."

Sheldon didn't comment. He wasn't much interested now. What was more important at this stage was the question of their chances of a safe return to Fort Phil Kearny — and whether the fort was still holding out.

On the morning of the twenty-eighth they decided to make a move. Snow was still coming down but gently, adding to the depth of the drifts but with less wind and a higher temperature. It would make travel difficult but would offer a margin of safety. War parties would not be out.

They returned by the route they had come — or as near to it as they could guess, not having known exactly where they were during most of the earlier trip. They traveled slowly but with no halts, aware that a wandering Indian might stumble upon their trail at any time and set up a pursuit. Twice they spotted hostile villages along the lower slopes of the ridge but no Indians seemed to be interested in the high country.

At dusk they could see Fort Phil Kearny from Fort Ridge. They could also see two Indian encampments in the valley below. "We didn't know how lucky we were the other night," Sheldon said as they stared at the snow-covered tepees. "I'd guess that we came right between those two villages on the way out. Even in the storm it was sheer luck that we weren't discovered."

"It seems to take a lot of luck to stay alive in this country," Pierce agreed. "A lot of luck that some of the boys didn't have."

They held their position until darkness closed down, then they advanced cautiously along a line that would swing them well around the Indian villages. It meant added distance but that was a small matter now.

Just before midnight they saw a glimmer of light ahead and almost at once heard the yell of alarm from a wagon-camp sentry. Both slid from their horses in a hurry, not knowing how nervous the picket might be. "Don't shoot!" Sheldon hailed. "Captain Pierce and Ross Sheldon coming in."

"Come ahead," a voice replied, relief apparent in the tone. "I'm glad it's not Injuns."

Sheldon chuckled. "At least we're not bottom choice."

"Don't start feeling proud," Pierce warned with an answering laugh. "When they get a smell of us we'll likely go down the list a notch or two."

Sheldon did not reply. He was thinking that the man beside him had changed a great deal in the past few weeks. Sam Hanna's "purty boy" had forgotten some of his interest in formality and brass buttons.

Their return brought no particular attention. Men who saw them come in seemed to think that they had been out on some sort of scouting trip. There were questions about the number of Indians around the fort but nothing more. Sheldon suddenly realized that the Crabiel-Enright affair meant little or nothing to men who had been living in their own atmosphere of grim danger.

Nor was this danger ended. The Sioux were still around the post, their offensive plans held up by the blizzard but still threatening. Whether John Phillips had got through to Fort Reno or to Laramie with the story of their plight was still unknown. Conditions were much as they had been on that brutal night of the twenty-first.

One change was in morale and Sheldon could sense it even as they passed through the guard lines. At the news of the Fetterman massacre the greener troops had been almost in a panic, held to their duty by the steadying influence of veteran comrades and by the prompt orders of the commanding officer. Now the panic was over. Men knew their proper posts and were getting accustomed to the dreary routine of manning them. The expected Sioux assault had not materialized and the defenders were becoming critical of the Indians for their laxity. A week earlier the garrison had steeled itself to fight to the death; now it expected to fight to victory if it had to fight at all. Many of the men insisted that the Indians had wasted their opportunity and would not make a real attempt to take the fort.

Non-military personnel shared that feeling. Women who had spent the night of the twenty-first consoling Mrs. Grummond had turned now to more practical duties. They were serving as nurses in the post hospital, attending to the wholesale cases of frostbite — which was threatening to disable the garrison in spite of all precautions.

Sheldon was taken to the hospital as soon as he arrived in the fort. The bruised ribs and forearms would heal without particular coddling but his chin, nose and left hand continued to give him pain. Pierce practically dragged him to the post surgeon, who treated him carefully and ordered him to bed.

The easing of his aches, plus a bit of hot soup in his stomach, sent him off into an exhausted slumber and he awakened to find the lamps lighted, the blackness of night showing at the one window within his range of vision. The sight puzzled him because he felt rested; it ought to be daylight by now.

He sat up in the bunk and almost immediately a woman's voice asked, "Is anything wrong?" He knew without turning his head that it was Harriet Winthrop who had spoken.

"Nothing important," he told her. "I'm just a bit confused. It seems like I've been asleep a long time but it's still night."

"But not the same night," she told him with a little smile. "You slept the clock around and a little more for good measure. I understand that Captain Pierce did the same thing."

"Then he's all right?"

"Fine. He seems to have stood the ordeal better than you did. I'm sorry if that injures your manly pride but it seems to be true."

By that time he knew that he was in a room of the post hospital and that other men were in the bunks around him. That made Miss Winthrop the nurse, of course. "I'll not be jealous," he told her with a grin that was brief because it hurt. "Pierce took better care of himself than I did."

Her smile faded. "Are you implying that he shirked his share of the duty?"

It annoyed him to realize that he should not have attempted such a subtle bit of humor. Other people would not know of his improved relations with Pierce. "My mistake," he said. "I shouldn't try to make jokes where you're concerned. You always come up with the worst possible interpretation."

"That sounds just like you! Making silly remarks and then trying to make me sound unreasonable because I fail to appreciate their sterling worth!"

"Here we go again," he groaned. "Is this Colonel Carrington's pet scheme for keeping men on duty — having a bad-tempered nurse to drive the boys back to the sentry posts?"

"Take it easy there, mister!" a voice called sharply. "You can't talk thataway to a lady what's doin' everything she can for us."

Sheldon grinned, catching the girl's look of triumph. "Sorry, boys," he replied. "She's your little angel of mercy, I suppose, but she's my pet earache. Don't mind the way we talk to each other; it's just a sort of old family feud."

She took a step toward him, eyes flashing. "Do you realize how you're making it sound?" she demanded in a sharp whisper. "What will these men think?"

He realized what she meant and for a moment had the grace to be embarrassed at his own blunder. Then he decided to carry out the attack. For once he had her on the run in an argument. It was too good an opportunity to lose.

"Don't try to hush me," he said aloud. "Your father insisted. It wasn't my idea, you know." That ought to hold her for a while!

For a moment he thought he was going to see a real display of temper. She flushed, stammered something that never became quite coherent — but turned to stalk out of the room. He had scored a clear-cut victory but he didn't feel very pleased with himself. It had been a dirty trick.

He rolled out of the bunk, found his clothes on a peg along the wall and dressed quickly, careful not to wipe off the ointment which had been smeared on his tender spots. Rest had done him a lot of good and he felt certain that none of his injuries was serious. In another couple of days he could forget all about them.

The other men in the room watched him without comment until he started to leave. Then a thin-faced young fellow snapped, "I hope you're goin' out to tell her you're sorry, mister. It ain't decent to hurt a fine lady like that one."

Sheldon halted at the door. "Forget what I said, friend. It didn't mean a thing." Then, he went on out.

He supposed that it was not entirely proper for him to discharge himself this way but he didn't think anyone would object. Harriet probably wouldn't even report him missing. She would simply be glad that he had gone.

He did not see her again for three days and he assumed that she was avoiding him deliberately. Nor could he blame her. During that period he found time to visit the wagon camp frequently, learning that the teamsters were enjoying their idleness. Some of the army's sawed planks were disappearing into the stoves as fires were kept up but it wasn't likely that anyone in authority would know or complain. The mules had suffered from the cold and three of them had died but for the most part they were in good condition.

"Keep them as fit as possible," he warned Prine. "If we get a relief column up from Laramie there's almost certain to be a return movement of some kind. I think we can get ourselves included in that return train."

"Suits me," Smoke told him. "Even Laramie will be some improvement over this ornery little outpost of the North Pole. Anyway I don't like the kind o' choruses the boys sing at me nowadays. They ain't real flatterin'."

CHAPTER
EIGHTEEN

New Year's Day was recognized in grim fashion, the garrison turning out in a memorial service for the victims of the Fetterman disaster. Then the frozen bodies were finally buried, the post taking some relief from the fact that the sad relics no longer haunted the parade ground.

In the evening there was a rather solemn social gathering at Colonel Carrington's quarters, and Sheldon found himself hauled along to it by Captain Pierce. By now the story of their exploit on Rock Creek was known among the officers although the reason behind the journey was still something of a mystery to them. The women knew only that Pierce had come to Powder River on a secret mission and that he had been able to carry out his orders by some rather unusual assistance on the part of Ross Sheldon. Being army wives they knew that they could not ask direct questions but most of them understood that Sheldon had become something of a hero. Pierce had made that point quite clear.

Partly because he felt uneasy at getting so much attention and partly because there was business to discuss, Sheldon drew Harriet Winthrop aside at the first opportunity. She was as cool as ever but made no protest, evidently not wishing to make a scene.

"I'm hoping to get our wagons out of here," he told her. "Do you want to go along or would you prefer to wait until better transportation is available in the spring?"

"I came on business," she replied, as terse as he was. "I'll go that way."

He explained his ideas and she nodded approval, discussing details in a completely impersonal manner. He noticed that most of the people in the room were watching them with some show of amusement but because he was engrossed in what he was saying he didn't realize at first that it was unusual. When he did notice it he was puzzled.

"What's wrong in here?" he asked with a frown. "I know Pierce has been spreading a lot of guff about how I saved his life — when I was as helpless as any man could be — but being a fake hero is no reason for everybody to stare at me with a big grin. What's wrong? Have I got a dirty face or something?"

"You mean you don't know?"

"If I did I wouldn't ask."

She smiled with disarming good humor. "That's the kind of remark to explain the whole thing. Either you get boorish in your manners or you let your perverted sense of humor run away with you."

He started to protest but thought better of it. "I suppose that sizes me up pretty good," he admitted, his grin slightly awry. "I'm not a nice character, but that's no reason for folks to keep staring at me as though they all wanted to rush over and pat me benevolently on my thick head. Some of those women look downright maternal."

"Their sentimental natures run away with them just as your warped humor runs away with you. Do you recall our last meeting?"

"Vaguely. We wrangled — of course. I seem to remember that I won — by playing you a dirty trick."

"An excellent description. I suppose you thought it was a very smart way to shut me up."

"Any way would be smart — if it would work."

"There you go again! Do you want to hear this or not?"

"My humble apologies. Go on."

"You deliberately embarrassed me by letting those men think we were married. There has been a lot of gossip."

"Holy Pete! I didn't . . . But I told those jackasses that it was just nonsense! They should have . . ." He broke off helplessly.

"Go on, Mister Sheldon. Stammer. I'm enjoying it. For once in your self-satisfied life you don't have a brilliant and cutting remark to make. This time you've opened your big mouth and put your foot in it. Go on and squirm!"

In spite of his discomfiture he had to laugh. "Go ahead and hammer me. I've got it coming."

"I intend to. In fact I've already started my campaign."

He didn't ask her what she meant. Instead he told her, "I'll tell them the truth. I started this mess so I'll have to clear it up."

"I'm afraid it's too late," she said quietly. "I tried to explain it but no one would believe me. They just smiled and assumed that we had been trying to hide our little secret all the time. So I changed my tactics. I hinted that you married me to get a job with my father's company. You now have something of a reputation at Fort Phil Kearny. You are so undependable that I had to come up here to see that you didn't get into trouble. The reason we don't see any more of each other than we do is because I'm so thoroughly disgusted with your general worthlessness and because you resent the necessary supervision that I have to force upon you. I'm getting the idea built up to the point where I'm almost a martyr to your bad qualities."

He stared at her in disbelief but the mocking smile told him that she was telling the truth. "You've been telling people that?" he exploded.

She smiled prettily. "I've been doing some neat hinting. I've been considering a stronger approach for this evening. I think I'll reprimand you here in public. That ought to teach you a good lesson."

He nodded, watching her eyes closely. "I think you'd do it," he told her slowly. "And I'll grant that it would be as fair a trick as mine. So I'll propose surrender terms. If you promise not to make me sound any worse than you have already done I'll promise not to go to Colonel Carrington."

Some of her smug satisfaction fell away as she asked, "What do you mean by that? Why should I care whether you, visit the Colonel?"

"I could apply to him for a change of quarters. With everybody in such a humorously romantic mood around here he might be sympathetic to a request that I be quartered with my wife."

Her long silence left him uneasy, a little afraid that now she might make a real scene. It was something of a relief when she met his glance again. "I crowed too soon," she admitted. "I should have remembered that you were a hard man to defeat. I accept the terms."

"Fair enough," he agreed. "It was nice fighting with you. Maybe we should mark the New Year on the calendar as the time both of us had to admit we were wrong. That hasn't happened very often, you know."

Her smile came again; he had decided to be good-humored about the whole ridiculous situation. "Maybe you're right. We've both been pretty mulish, I'm sure."

"And what about the gossip? Want me to have a try at straightening it out?"

"I'm afraid it would be useless. Anyway it's something for the poor souls to enjoy, something to take their minds away from the tragedies around them. We'll be out of here before long, if your plan works out, and I don't mind letting them have their fun. Until the wagons get away we'll just see each other on business and otherwise stay away. Let them make what they will of it."

"Shucks!" he complained. "I was just beginning to like it."

She threw him a warning frown and he looked up to see two ladies bearing down on them, clearly intent on breaking up the tete-a-tete.

"Are we interrupting?" the stouter woman asked, her voice and expression indicating that she felt certain that they were.

Sheldon gave her his most formal bow. "No interruption, ma'am. Miss Winthrop and I were just clearing up a matter of business. Her father and I are business partners, you know."

He did not give her a chance to express the cheerful disbelief which was evident in her eyes. Turning to Harriet Winthrop he went on briskly, "I'll let you know how I make out in that matter, ma'am. We'll have to take our chances with the weather but I'll have all of the wagons ready if the opportunity comes along."

"Thank you, Mr. Sheldon," she replied, her tone almost a duplicate of his. "I trust your judgment in the matter. Good evening." There was a suggestion of droop to one of her eyelids as she spoke the words and he turned away, suppressing a grin. Maybe it would be just as much fun to have her on his side in these little battles of wits as it was to be against her. It could even be better that way.

On the following, morning a party of scouts probed cautiously into the hills east of the fort while a squadron of mounted infantry rode out to the crest of the Sullivant Hills. Both parties reported substantially the same condition. The besieging Indians had withdrawn from the immediate vicinity of the fort. The fact that they had moved their villages in the midst of a blizzard was as big a mystery as the reason for their apparent abandonment of the siege.

"Injun nature," Chief Scout Bailey grunted when the question was raised at the wagon barracks. "Injuns ain't good campaigners. Set 'em to screechin' around a wagon train or a trapped column and there ain't no better fighters nowhere. But give 'em a job that takes organization or patience and they ain't got it."

"They had it last summer and fall," Sheldon pointed out. "What happened since then?"

"Hard to tell. The way I figger it Red Cloud and Crazy Horse had 'em lined up real good. They watched their chances and trapped Fetterman. That was when they had us in the bag, but they didn't pull the string. Mebbe it was because they jest had to ack like Injuns and hold up a spell to make medicine. Fisher and Wheatly hurt 'em bad in that fight so mebbe they went back to their lodges fer the usual weepin' and wailin'. One way or another they blew their big chance. Before Red Cloud could whip 'em up to a fightin' mood again the blizzard hit 'em. A week o' that and they kinda lost heart. Injuns ain't much fer winter fightin', ye know."

General opinion agreed with him. Three days later a relief column came in from Laramie by way of Fort Reno, reporting that there had been no attacks and that the trail to the south was virtually clear of hostiles. Lieutenant-Colonel Wessels, in command of the new troops, also reported the amazing feat of John Phillips in fighting his way into Laramie. He had staggered into the midst of a Christmas party with the message from Phil Kearny after the ride of two hundred and sixty miles through the blizzard. His horse had died at the gate of the fort and Phillips was still in the hospital.

Wessels had a variety of orders, one of them being to organize a force that would strike at the winter-bound Indian villages. The hard-riding Sioux could not follow their usual slashing tactics in deep snow and it was felt that the better equipped soldiers would thus gain an advantage. It was a virtual admission that in good weather and on his own ground the Sioux was too tough.

"It makes sense," Sheldon told Pierce, "although I don't envy the men who make the campaign. However, the point is that this could be the reason the Indians have pulled back from the fort. We know they keep in touch with our posts through the renegade traders who sell them guns and whiskey. Maybe they get information from the same sources. It's possible they've had warning of this plan."

Pierce nodded. "I'll mention it in my report. If I'm lucky somebody else can run down the idea. I've had about all I can take of this country."

"Buck up!" Sheldon laughed. "You'll take a lot more of it before we see Laramie. It's a long haul, and we haven't had any snow for two days. That kind of good weather can't last."

They had been making preparations even before the arrival of Wessels's men. Carrington had readily agreed to the departure of the Sheldon wagons, making it official by assigning them to transport some of the sick and wounded back to Laramie. With the apparent raising of the siege there was no point in keeping extra men around who would be only a drain on the commissary.

The wagon crews busied themselves with the job of getting wagon boxes remounted and equipping the best wagons as ambulances. Harriet Winthrop had expressed her firm determination to go with the train, so a wagon was fitted up as living quarters for her. Like most of the ambulances it was equipped with a small stove and as many other comforts as possible.

There was some delay in getting good teams selected. Ailing mules had to be exchanged for sound ones, either by trade with the post authorities or with other contractors. Finally, however, plans were completed and a tentative starting date was set.

Then Wessels's columns arrived and there was an extra day of delay as Colonel Carrington requested a change in the plan. There were twenty men in the fort due for discharge and he proposed that they accompany the train to Laramie, taking over its guard duty and the care of the wounded men. That suited Sheldon fine. Twenty veterans with the train would be a great help.

The reinforcement didn't cause him to relax his care. It was important to get started without being observed so they planned to move at night. The second day after Wessels's arrival was clear and cold so they decided to move at dusk, figuring on a first quarter moon to make night travel possible. With some six hours of moonlight in prospect the train should be clear of any Indian pickets before having to halt for the dark part of the night. Last minute prepaartions were made and just before sunset Harriet came out to the wagon camp, bringing her scanty luggage.

Sheldon was not there to greet her because he had spent the last hour of daylight at the office of the new chief quartermaster, General Dandy, closing out the accounts of the wagon train. He had tried to have the chore handled by Harriet but Dandy had refused, winking broadly as he chuckled, "No use making pretenses with me, Sheldon. I know you're a tricky one but the cat's out of the bag. You might as well handle it yourself and not bother your wife; she has a hard journey ahead of her."

"But I . . ."

"No protests, sir. You will remember that I was a small party to some of your sharp practices back at Laramie so don't try to sound innocent. You're just as bad as Rowdy Russell — bless his heart! Now help me out with these accounts that poor Brown left unfinished."

It took a long time. In addition to the regular contracts there are separate deals involving the handling of army wagons with the contract train, several exchanges of rations and finally the deal with the mules. Eventually General Dandy was satisfied that everything was perfectly in order and he issued the proper warrants against government authorities at Laramie and at Leavenworth. When Sheldon arrived at the wagon camp the wagoners and their escort were eating supper, the whole detachment ready to move as soon as the sun went down.

Sheldon ate with Smoke and Pierce, discovering that Pierce was uneasy over having been put in charge of the military command. Brown had been the only officer slated for transfer so Pierce had to be commanding officer.

"You're the train captain, of course," he told Sheldon. "I assume no authority over anything. The men under my orders know more about this business than I do — and they know that they know. I'll report them in formally at Laramie but on the trail their real commander will be Corporal Tanner. Corporal Jenkins is in charge of the sick detail."

Sheldon grinned. "Corporal Tanner is the former rebel who gave us the information on Enright, in case you didn't remember. Don't you think it might sound peculiar that you made a field commander of him?"

"I don't care how it sounds," Pierce replied with a small grin. "It wouldn't make any difference to me right now if Tanner had been a Rebel general. He's the man for the job. I'm not."

"Have it your way. We'll move in another fifteen minutes. Better pass the word to Tanner. While we're still on the post you ought to make motions as though you were running the party."

Pierce grinned amiably and Sheldon moved away, going over to the big wagon that was to be Harriet Winthrop's conveyance. The front canvas was parted and he could see that she was inside, eating her supper by the light of a suspended lantern.

"About ready to leave," he announced briskly. "I brought along a half-ton of official papers. You'd better put them in a safe place; they're our claim to the profits for the whole expedition."

"Nothing went wrong, I hope," she said. "I was a little afraid that Captain Brown might have left some of the accounts in a mess."

He shook his head, watching her closely. "Brown didn't let his personal interests interfere with his duty, I imagine. His accounts were in order."

"I'm glad to hear it. I liked Captain Brown. I wouldn't want to have my memory of him affected by any feeling that he had left us with legal troubles."

"The only trouble was mine," he told her. "General Dandy insisted on charging me for one Spencer carbine that I borrowed and did not return. Since he let us trade even on the mules — which was all in our favor — I didn't object."

"What objection could you make? You were responsible for the loss of an army weapon."

"I could enter a counter-claim for having brought back one reasonably good captain in place of the busted carbine."

"I'm surprised that you didn't," she said quietly. "We can deduct the gun charge from your share of the profits."

"Fair enough. It should just about balance the charge I'll have to make for transporting one non-working passenger from Kearny to Laramie."

She let the smile come then. "I think we're involved in another deadlock, Captain. Maybe we should avoid all of the unnecessary bookkeeping and ignore both charges. After all, your great modesty in not claiming credit for Captain Pierce is worth something. Rare items usually have considerable value."

He grinned broadly in the gathering dusk. "We're off to a fine belligerent start. Better pull down the flaps before we start to move out. It's going to get cold tonight."

CHAPTER
NINETEEN

A perfect half-moon hung in the southern sky, paled by the lingering red of the sunset beyond the Big Horns, when the wagons moved out along the beaten trail left by Wessels's men. Scouts reported everything clear to the south but flankers went out just the same.

The night had fallen still and cold but the air was crisp rather than bitter as wagon wheels crunched the frozen snow, the peculiar squeak-squeak of hoofs and iron tires almost the only sound to break the wintry silence. Here and there a man coughed or swore softly at his mules but it was mostly a quiet march, everyone fully aware of the need for caution.

The already packed trail made travel fairly easy, the combination of the moon and a wavering greenish Aurora Borealis making the night almost too bright for safety. On such a night the hostiles might be wandering around.

At midnight they had left Lake De Smet well behind, nothing having interrupted the steady march. By that time the moon was dipping behind the peaks of the Big Horns but the brilliance of the northern lights on snow was still sufficient so that Sheldon did not call a halt. This was the critical part of the trip. Once clear of the area where the hostiles had gathered during the past three months they would be comparatively safe.

The train finally corraled at one-thirty, guards being posted with orders for relief every hour. Anyone not having duty found a place in one of the wagons, getting extra protection from the cold by burrowing into the piles of buffalo robes that had been distributed through the train.

That had been Smoke's idea. Two full loads of hides were being hauled to Laramie for trade but on the way they were being used as bedding. Men could crawl in among them and keep fairly warm. They didn't make the sweetest-smelling beds in the world but at ten below zero nobody cared.

At six o'clock the entire company rolled out. Sheldon had planned a two-hour march before making a breakfast halt but to his surprise and satisfaction he found that Harriet Winthrop had been brewing coffee in her wagon. By using the stove there she had avoided the risk that would have been attendant upon the lighting of open fires. Smoke passed the word and within a few minutes every man in the train except the guards and the wounded were gathering for a small coffee ration.

She had contrived to brew two pots full but it still meant only a swallow or two for each man, especially when Corporal Jenkins insisted on giving each of his invalid charges a little more than their proper share. Still it sent all hands to their duties in a good mood and the advance began promptly.

Harriet was almost apologetic when the coffee ran out. "I didn't have utensils enough," she told Sheldon. "Do you suppose it would be all right for me to brew some more while the wagons are moving?"

Sheldon shook his head. "You'd only scald yourself or set fire to the wagon. The guards who didn't get any coffee are snug under buffalo hides since they went off duty so they'll get along until we stop for a real breakfast. The important thing is that the men now going on duty have a bit of warmth inside."

"Then it was all right for me to do it?"

"You've earned your passage already," he told her. "I take back what I said about non-working passengers. You are now the commissary officer."

"Careful," she warned. "You'll spoil me with such rare praise."

He smiled easily. "A week ago I probably would have made some answer about it being too late to spoil you. Now that we've decided to act almost human I'll try to maintain the reform. So I won't say it."

She laughed aloud. "That's the sort of reform program I might have expected from you. You become gallant by explaining how ungallant you might have been. Why don't you stop trying so hard, Ross Sheldon?"

"Trying? What do you mean?"

"Just what I said. Captain Brown and I talked about you one evening and he mentioned that you and he had held a similar discussion. We decided that the three of us had a lot in common. We try too hard to be what each of us thought we wanted to be. I have been so

218

anxious to prove that I can be the kind of business woman my father feared I would not be that I sometimes make myself pretty unpleasant. You have been so keen on proving that you could handle the responsibility which your military assignment denied you that you become rather annoying in your attempts to be right all the time. Captain Brown — but we'll not discuss that part."

"Nice speech," he told her with a smile. "If you talked to Brown you know that I've been trying to say something of the sort. Maybe this will be another great shock to you but I agree completely. I'll stop trying if you will."

"A bargain," she agreed. "From now on no nasty remarks — unless delivered with a smile."

He nodded silently as Smoke appeared, climbing to the wagon seat and launching into a tirade at the mules. It was noteworthy that Prine had provided himself with a whole new vocabulary since becoming the driver of Miss Winthrop's wagon. He had invented a string of words which were quite meaningless but which conceivably might sound like profanity to mules. At least, the mules moved out as briskly as though they had been cussed properly.

Sheldon stood in the snow, chuckling. After a while he realized that Smoke's performance was not as amusing as all that. He was just chuckling because he felt happy. In something like embarrassment he hurried away and climbed into the saddle. It was no time for a train captain to be getting that kind of ideas.

Again they made good time, halting once in mid-morning for the delayed breakfast and again in the afternoon as they approached the ridge country along Crazy Woman Fork. When scouts reported that the stream had no hostile villages along it they pushed forward, making camp in the shelter of a bluff.

It was a comfortable night, the thermometer in the back of Harriet's wagon going almost up to zero. After so much colder weather that seemed merely brisk. In the morning Smoke became Miss Winthrop's assistant and the coffee ration became something of a ceremony. It was a small matter but it made for good spirits among the men.

The trail was still easy, no quantity of snow having fallen since the passage of Wessels's troops. An advance guard rode a short distance ahead of the train while another pair of soldiers watched the rear, but no flankers were sent out. The deep snow on both sides seemed to make it unnecessary.

Two hours after leaving Crazy Woman Fork, however, Sheldon left the train to send his mule floundering through the snow toward a line of ridges. He had got a glimpse of a herd of buffalo in that direction and there was a restlessness among the animals which made him suspicious. Within a few minutes he understood it. A party of twenty mounted men were moving toward the herd, evidently with designs upon it. At the distance Sheldon could only guess that they were Indians. All were so muffled in furs that nothing could be distinguished, but their style of riding seemed to mark them as Sioux or Cheyennes. It puzzled him a little that he couldn't see any lances among them but it was not an important point.

He watched without disclosing his own position, making certain that the party was indeed intending to strike at the buffalo. Then he rode back down the ridge to the wagons, passing the word that they were to be ready for defense at short notice. With the snowbanks along both sides of the trail it would take a little longer than usual to go into corral so he wanted them ready.

"We're not now in their sight," he told Pierce and Tanner. "If the herd breaks to the west we'll probably not be discovered. If the chase turns east we may have double trouble, both with the buffalo and also because the Indians will be sure to spot us."

"You think they'll attack us?" Pierce asked.

"Likely. They're real proud of themselves now, you know. I think we'll do well to bait them into an attack — if they see us at all."

"That's askin' fer trouble," Corporal Tanner protested. "Some of us boys are lookin' forward to gettin' outa this mess with a whole hide. We ain't keen on messin' up in a Injun fight this close to discharge day."

"Lieutenant Sheldon gives the orders!" Pierce snapped, stressing the title. "He knows this business better than we do."

Sheldon let the quick grin come and go. He was reminded of the day when Colonel Carrington had given him military rank for purposes of impressing Pierce. Now Pierce was using the same trick.

"You know I'm no glory hunter," he told Tanner. "And I'm very much aware of the fact that we've got a woman and some wounded men with us. But we've got to face facts. It would be foolhardy to put our men in the saddle as skirmishers and we can't let the enemy hang on our flanks all the way to Laramie. I figure that our best bet is to play their own pet trick on them. Let them think we're weak and then hit them hard when they attack. If we hurt them bad enough they'll not try us again."

Tanner grinned wryly. "I ain't goin' to argue, Lieutenant. Sorry I sounded off. What's the order?"

"Keep all of your men in the wagons except those needed to take care of the extra animals. When I give the signal to fort up get everybody out of sight and behind good solid protection where it's possible. You and Captain Pierce can work out details; I'm going back on picket."

He paused at Smoke's wagon long enough to tell Harriet what was in mind. "Your assignment is to lie down on the bottom of the wagon," he told her. "Stay between those boxes as much as you can. Stray bullets can be just as deadly as any other kind."

"I'll load while Prine shoots," she said calmly. "We have two rifles with us, you know."

"Then load lying down," he retorted. "If we have a fight the men will want some coffee when it's over. Can't afford to lose the coffee detail."

He rode back up the ridge then, not even looking back when she called something to him which he could not quite make out.

When he sighted the Indians they were much closer, the buffalo herd having drifted toward the southeast at increasing speed. That would take them across the Reno trail well ahead of the wagons but there was flat country just ahead and when the pursuers of the herd reached that area there would no longer be any ridge to screen the wagon train.

He held his flanking position for another fifteen minutes, keeping well below the crest so that he could watch the Indians and still remain out of their sight. He didn't suppose that they could see him even if they looked in the right direction. He was almost up-sun from them and the glare on the snow would put him squarely in their blind spot.

Then the ridge dwindled away and the lumbering herd swung hard to the east. In another minute or two the wagons would be discovered. He gave Pierce the signal and turned back, watching the wagons close up into their tight little box with the extra stock in the center.

It was a neat little maneuver and he felt pride to see it handled so well. Then he looked back over his shoulder just in time to see one of the Indians gesticulating wildly. The train had been discovered.

It didn't take the savages long to forget the buffalo. They whirled their horses and drove down upon their intended victims, a couple of them firing long-range shots at Sheldon.

The little huddle of wagons did not look very sturdy, Sheldon thought as he approached them. Two mounted men rode around the outer rim of the corral as though hesitant about their next moves but no one else moved. The confident Sioux would not suspect that a score of grim veterans lay there with rifles ready, sided by experienced teamsters who had just as much reason as the soldiers to want revenge on the Indians.

Sheldon rode into the corral, motioning for the two soldiers to follow him. By that time the Indians were getting close enough so that some of the details of their equipment could be seen. Every one of them carried a carbine or a rifle. That explained the absence of any lances. This band was particularly well armed.

"How are the men distributed, Corporal?" Sheldon called as he slid from his mule.

"Spaced as even as we could git 'em, Lieutenant."

"Better make some shifts. Reinforce the head of the train and the east side. Keep only two or three at the rear and two on the right"

"But the varmints are comin' in from the southwest."

"They're not stupid. They'll want the sun at their back When they attack. They've got guns and they'll want to see what they're shooting at."

Tanner threw a salute and hustled away to issue new orders. Sheldon noted that the men made the change stealthily, not betraying themselves to the advancing enemy.

They were making grim preparations all along the line, men laying out extra cartridges on wagon seats or wherever it was most convenient. Sheldon hoped that each man had plenty of shells. With at least four kinds of weapons being used by the troops and as many more in the hands of the wagoners there could be no general scheme for supplying ammunition.

224

He circled the defense line, warning every man to hold his fire until the enemy was committed to their assault. "Let 'em get close. Wait until I fire the first shot. Then pour it in! With any luck we'll wipe 'em out."

The corral fell silent except for the braying of the mules, and the Sioux came closer, angling forward a little so as to strike the beaten trail a hundred yards ahead of the spot where the train had stopped. There they split, a dozen of them riding around to the east while the remainder huddled in the path.

Tanner turned to grin at Sheldon who was behind him, peering out between number one and number two wagons. "Looks like you called the turn, Colonel. Want me to bring the other men over here?"

"Leave them for reserve in case any of the devils manage to break into the corral. Not that I think they will."

"Right again, Colonel. Mebbe I'll git it in my thick head purty soon that you're a jump ahead o' me all the time."

Sheldon chuckled. "At the rate you're promoting me I'll be a jump ahead of General Sherman before the day is over."

Tanner's voice was low as he said, "I was a major back in the old days. I kinda like to take my orders from a man what out-ranks me. That's just between the two of us, you understand."

"Thanks for the confidence. Let's get ready."

The admonition wasn't needed. All along the line men were laying cheeks to gunstocks and shielding eyes from the sun's glare as they watched the savages wheel into their line of attack.

It was not to be the slashing sort of charge so characteristic of the Plains Indian, evidently because the depth of snow made such an attack impossible. The raiders simply fanned out along the east side of the trail until a gunshot sounded from the group that had remained on the beaten trail. Then they sent their ponies plunging toward the wagons, the one group concentrating on the head of the corral while the others drove for openings along the side.

CHAPTER
TWENTY

Sheldon held his fire until the charging warriors were within a hundred feet. Then he began to empty his Colt into the galloping ranks. A rattle of fire that was almost a volley told him that ready trigger fingers had been alert for his signal. Half of the Sioux in front of him went sprawling at the first burst of fire — and then the teamsters opened up. They had reserved their fire until the soldiers had slammed in the first withering blast.

The charge faltered and broke, dismayed survivors trying to halt the headlong pace to turn and escape. Horses went down, either by gunfire or by skidding on the icy crust as their riders tried to turn them. Here and there an Indian tried to discharge his rifle but the defense fire was deadly, the sprinkling of repeating weapons maintaining the pressure while other men reloaded.

A single warrior broke through between the wagons midway along the line but was blasted to the snow by the reserves on the west side. By that time the trail ahead of the train was a mass of twisted bodies, none of them moving for many seconds. Wounded Indians were dangerous and the memory of dead comrades was too strong for any of the defenders to waste sentiment. Anything that moved drew a bullet.

Sheldon did not even find time to reload his Colt. As he fired his last shot he knew that the force in front of him had been completely wiped out. A few shots were still sounding along the side of the train as men tried to stop two Indians who had managed to turn their ponies and ride away. Otherwise the skirmish was over in one swift outpouring of vengeful lead.

Cheering burst out all along the line, broken only by the disgusted cursing of men who blamed themselves for the escape of the two lucky Indians. Sheldon let them whoop it up for a few minutes, knowing that they had it coming. After being on the defensive for so long it was their right to exult over a victory. He was even glad that a couple of the enemy had escaped. The story they would take back to the villages would be worth plenty to other whites along the Bozeman Trail.

Finally he shouted them down, issuing quick orders. "Wagons get ready to move; check your teams! Captain Pierce, will you have your men detailed to the usual duties of inspecting enemy dead, sir?"

Pierce was already on his feet, smiling in a somewhat dazed fashion. He blinked a little at the reminder that he had a duty to perform but recovered himself to shout, "Corporal Tanner. Send out the detail. Salvage all possible weapons. Identify any enemy you can. We'll want to know all we can about them. Also see if we have any casualties."

There was a flat silence before a teamster straightened up from where he had been bending over

228

in the snow. "Looks like poor Tanner got it, Cap'n," he said bleakly. "Slug took him right twixt the eyes."

Sheldon stepped into the breach. "Four men over here," he snapped. "Help Captain Pierce with Tanner's body." He singled out a burly soldier who looked as though he might be getting suddenly sick. "You — take four other men and go take a look at the bodies along the east side. You men there by number four wagon come with me."

He refused to look down at the fallen Tanner, pushing out between the lead wagons to inspect the dead Indians in the trail. It was no time for sentiment. The trail had to be cleared so that the train could push on toward the temporary protection of Fort Reno, so bodies were flung into the snowbanks with something akin to savagery. If there was life in any of the fallen forms no one wanted to know it. Tanner's death had stilled their enthusiasm for victory, leaving them with the old bitterness.

Sheldon saw the work started but then went back to the wagons, sending a couple of men out on horseback to shoot the few Indian ponies that still floundered in the snow. There was no time to catch the unwounded ones so the only sensible thing was to make sure that no warrior would ever ride them again.

He knew now that the raiders had been a mixed gang of Oglalas and Arapahoes, probably outlaws even from their own villages. All of them had been armed with brand new Henry repeaters and the sight of so many fine weapons almost gave him the chills. The successful ambush had been the only thing that had saved the train. If the Indians had elected to skirmish at long range with those rifles they might have cut the defenders to pieces.

"Lucky I was fearful of those buffalo," he told Pierce when they met by the wagons. "Maybe I wouldn't have tried the ambush if I hadn't been afraid of getting skirmishers caught in a stampede. Because I had to figure on that buffalo risk I was forced into making the smart move. Dumb luck!"

"Luck for us," Pierce corrected. "Luck that you were giving the orders, I mean."

"Any other casualties?" Sheldon asked in a hurry.

"One of the men got a scratch on the point of his shoulder. He's in Miss Winthrop's wagon getting bandaged now — and liking it. She's as calm as ever. Got coffee about ready, I understand."

There was an interruption then as the detail from the east side came in, dragging something that looked like a bundle of buffalo robes. "Found one that ain't a redskin, sir," the burly trooper reported, saluting. "We figgered you'd want to have a look at him."

They dropped the dead man, rolling him over and brushing the snow from a swarthy face. Sheldon took one look at the black whiskers and heavy brows. Then he nodded toward Pierce. "That ought to help with your chore, Captain. This is one Jean Moreau. He works sometimes for John Richards and sometimes for Joe Bissonette. I think we can guess where those new rifles came from."

Pierce squatted beside the dead man and went through his clothing, coming up with several papers.

230

He did not look at them but thrust them into his own pocket. "Evidence," he muttered. "It might tell us something when we piece all of the facts together."

"Those new rifles ought to tell something," Sheldon reminded him. "The numbers on them should permit the shipment to be traced. It's a cinch that it was a recent one."

"Coffee here!" Miss Winthrop's voice called.

"Get it down fast, men," Sheldon advised. "We're moving in five minutes."

"We put Corporal Tanner's body in Gaylord's wagon," Pierce said in a low voice. "They'll give him decent burial at Reno."

"Do me a favor," Sheldon asked in the same tone. "Request the commander there to detail a burial squad of former Confederates, if he has any in the post. Let them know that they're doing the honors for Major Tanner."

"I'll make it clear," Pierce promised.

They pulled into Fort Reno just after dusk with a light snow falling. Sheldon was glad to have Pierce take care of all military formalities. This would be the only real stop short of Laramie so he wanted to make sure that all teams and equipment were ready for the long haul.

Miss Winthrop went into the fort on arrival, welcomed by several young officers who vied for the honor of greeting her. Sheldon assumed that she would seize the opportunity to spend a night under a roof but just as he was completing his chores she came out to the wagon camp, escorted by two lieutenants. He heard her thank them for their escort, her voice carrying a definite ring of dismissal. Then she came toward him in the semi-gloom that was compounded of moonlight shining through low scudding snow clouds.

"Sleeping in the wagon?" he asked.

"Of course. I would be an inconvenience to them inside. My quarters in the wagon are quite satisfactory."

"Very well. We'll be leaving early so it's easier that way."

"I wanted to tell you something," she went on, her voice dropping a little. "Captain Pierce has made it very plain that you saved us today. It was your idea to fight the kind of battle that was fought. He says that any other strategy would have been fatal to all of us."

"Pierce gets some pretty wild ideas," he laughed. "He's just trying to butter me up in compensation for those charges he made against me last summer."

"The officers here at Fort Reno agree with him. So do our men. Pierce has filed a formal report giving you full credit."

"Great!" he said dryly. "I spend four years of a war trying to get a chance to prove that I could be a soldier and all I do is play nursemaid to mail wagons. Now that I'm trying to be a good business man I suddenly turn out to be a military genius. What kind of medal do they give to muleskinners?"

"Now don't try to sound like your old self! Remember the agreement."

His laugh was a little easier. "I'll remember. You make it easier now. You're being a pretty good soldier yourself — for a girl whose only ambition in life was to show her father that she could boss a trading post."

"I guess we all change a little," she agreed. "At least we do if we ever grow up. Anyway I wanted to tell you that what you did was appreciated. By all of us."

He tried to cover his embarrassment by asking, "Then I won't have to have the cost of that Spencer deducted from my share? We can't offset it against your passage now that you're a working member of the crew."

"It's a bargain," she said solemnly. "I suppose it was worth it, although my private opinion is that you could afford the charge. I saw you appropriate a couple of those captured Henrys this afternoon."

"Legitimate share of the loot," he retorted.

"Agreed. I won't even lay claim to them for partnership." She turned quickly and went to her wagon, leaving him to stand for a long time with the snow drifting down around him. Maybe she was right about people changing. He knew that he had changed a lot of his own ideas within the past few weeks, even within the past few days.

At dawn the snow was still light and the train moved out without particular difficulty. Two army wagons from Reno went with them, along with the mail detail, thus giving them additional manpower for possible troubles.

The march proved uneventful, however, only a couple of heavy snowfalls adding to the difficulties of travel. Three days saw them at Willow Creek and on the fourth night they were across the North Platte, the traders in the area reporting no recent Indian activities.

Sheldon saw little of Harriet except at breakfast. She continued her coffee routine and was pampered by every man in the train. Immediately after leaving Reno he had organized daily hunting parties to range out from the trail, figuring that the fresh meat they might bring in would be as valuable as the scouting service they were also providing. Their luck was generally good and it became something of a contest to see which hunters could bring the choicest cuts to Miss Winthrop.

Heavy snow caught them at the new telegraph station at Horseshoe Creek but they did not delay. The train had something to keep up its morale and no man wanted to admit that they could not overcome any obstacle. Not only had they almost exterminated a band of Indians but they had to keep up a good appearance for a pretty girl who gave them coffee every morning.

The final day's march was probably the worst of the journey, a real blizzard hitting them with the temperature going to thirty below. Still they slogged through, soldiers relieving the regular drivers so that each man could take a turn in the shelter of the wagons when he wasn't needed to shovel some unfortunate vehicle out of a drift. There was still a little daylight left to them when they plowed past the fort at Laramie, the troops having left the wagons so as to ride into the post with some show of military order. At the gate Pierce had them face about and shout a farewell salute to the girl, who had climbed to the wagon seat. She waved in

234

return and the train rolled on to the shelter of the now completed Winthrop buildings. Even with their covering of new snow they looked snug and warm.

They found the trading post doing a bit of business under the watchful eye of Eli Ludlam but the freight corrals were almost bare of wagons and men, all equipment having been sent East for the next spring's hauling. It meant that tired drivers had to take care of their own equipment before getting a rest but they were used to it and made no complaints. An extra hour of labor meant nothing now.

Sheldon made sure that everything was squared away outside and then he went into the store, where a few curious folk had already gathered to hear the news of Fort Phil Kearny. Sheldon answered a few questions before Harriet came to the door of what appeared to be an office, signaling for him to join her.

She had used her time well, discarding the furs of the trail for a woolen gown that was suitable to the cold weather but which still served to remind him that she was a very attractive woman. He was suddenly conscious of his bushy whiskers and general unkempt appearance.

"I've checked the cash," she announced, "and there's plenty to meet a payroll. If you'll send the men in I'll pay them. They shouldn't be kept waiting after all they've gone through."

He nodded, turning back into the store without comment. Smoke Prine had just come in so Sheldon passed the orders on to him. "Send 'em in one at a time," he instructed. "I'm going to get cleaned up a bit."

Smoke winked. "I ain't blamin' ye, Ross. If I was in your boots I'd purty myself up all I could."

"Rats!" Sheldon snapped. "Miss Winthrop and I have a lot of accounts to go over. I don't want her to have to smell me in a warm room."

Smoke winked again, his grin showing the missing teeth even more than usual. "Say it your way; I'll think it mine."

Forty minutes later Sheldon returned to the office, feeling a little less like a bear just out of hibernation. Bathing facilities were pretty crude, especially with the temperature below zero, but he had shivered through the ordeal, getting enough hot water to shave.

Harriet smiled cordially when he came in. "I wondered what had happened to you," she said. "I didn't know you planned to become a dude."

"You shamed me into it. I figured if water wouldn't hurt you I could stand it too. Want to go over the accounts now?"

"Later will do. The men have all been paid and we'll have a couple of months before we can carry on any new business. There's no hurry."

"Your father will want a report by the mail."

"I'm sure he will. I've been reading several letters from him that have been waiting here. I'm not sure whether he is more angry at me for going to Powder River or more concerned for fear I'll do something to drive you away from the partnership. He's really

236

convinced that you're exactly the man to handle this end of the business."

"I've still got Cope to consider, you know."

"He seems to have settled that point. Cope is to be a partner, also, in charge of the wagon trains between here and the Missouri. Father intends to handle the Eastern end of the business while it lasts, leaving you to take full charge at this end."

"Sounds like he figured on every angle but yours. What happens to your ambition to be a business woman?"

"On that point he only hints. The idea seems to be that I operate the store here — if I can do it without interfering with your operations. I'm sure my father thinks that my greatest value to the company will be in keeping you from leaving it."

She avoided his eyes as she spoke the words and he made his voice elaborately casual as he replied, "Sounds like he's a real smart man. Got any ideas about how you're going to keep from wounding my tender feelings?"

"I'm not supposed to have ideas," she murmured. "That seems to be your department."

He sighed. "Then we're stuck. I don't have any new ideas either."

She looked up quickly, a frown puckering her brows. Sheldon added hastily, "No *new* ideas, I said. Maybe we could use an old one, the one I scared you with back at Phil Kearny, the one about telling Colonel Carrington that we were married."

The frown faded as swiftly as it had come. "It sounds possible," she said with a judicial air. "But I wasn't scared. I didn't think you would have the nerve to carry out the bluff."

"Still think I don't have the nerve?"

Before she could reply there was a familiar plinking of banjo strings from the store and Smoke's nasal tenor broke into song.

> We went to Powder River just to haul a load of
>   wood.
> The Injuns tried to scalp us — and they would
>   have if they could.
> Now Red Cloud's gang won't be so brash; we gave
>   'em all a pain.
> They got theirselves a bellyful of Sheldon's wagon
>   train.

Harriet didn't wait to hear the chorus. Nodding significantly toward the other room she murmured, "Smoke seems to be giving you credit for something that could be called nerve. Who am I to argue with Smoke?"

Sheldon reached for her. "Forget Smoke. I'm the one you're not supposed to argue with. Remember?"

She didn't argue.